# ALSO BY JIM HEYNEN

# THE ONE-ROOM SCHOOLHOUSE

# THE ONE-ROOM SCHOOLHOUSE

Stories About the Boys

## JIM HEYNEN

Alfred A. Knopf   New York   1993

THIS IS A BORZOI BOOK

PUBLISHED BY ALFRED A. KNOPF, INC.

COPYRIGHT © 1993 BY JIM HEYNEN

Some of the stories in this book were previously
published, in a slightly different form, in
ZYZZYVA; others appeared in *You Know What Is
Right* (North Point Press). "Bloating and Its
Remedies," "Who Made Such Good Pies" (now
"Pies"), "The Minister's Wife," "The First-Calf
Heifer," "What Started Walking Home from
School" (now "Walking Home from School"), "Who
Built a Lot of Sheds" (now "Sheds"), and "Spring
Grass," from *The Man Who Kept Cigars in His Cap*
by Jim Heynen, are published by permission of
Graywolf Press. "Electricity," "One Dead Chicken,"
"House Visitation," "The Forest," "The Dream,"
"What If," and "The Harvest" were originally
published in *The Georgia Review*.

Library of Congress Cataloging-in-Publication Data

Heynen, Jim, [date]
The one-room schoolhouse : stories about the
boys / Jim Heynen. — 1st ed.
p.   cm.
ISBN 0-679-41786-9
1. Country life—Iowa—Fiction.   I. Title.
PS3558.E8705   1993
813'.54—dc20                          92-54805
CIP

Manufactured in the United States of America

FIRST EDITION

FOR EMILY AND GEOFFREY

# CONTENTS

## PART V    GOTCHA

# WHAT HAPPENED
# DURING THE ICE STORM

One winter there was a freezing rain. How beautiful! people said when things outside started to shine with ice. But the freezing rain kept coming. Tree branches glistened like glass. Then broke like glass. Ice thickened on the windows until everything outside blurred. Farmers moved their livestock into the barns, and most animals were safe. But not the pheasants. Their eyes froze shut.

Some farmers went ice-skating down the gravel roads with clubs to harvest pheasants that sat helplessly in the roadside ditches. The boys went out into the freezing rain to find pheasants too. They saw dark spots along a fence. Pheasants, all right. Five or six of them. The boys slid their feet along slowly, trying not to break the ice that covered the snow. They slid up close to the pheasants. The pheasants pulled their heads down between their wings. They couldn't tell how easy it was to see them huddled there.

The boys stood still in the icy rain. Their breath came out in slow puffs of steam. The pheasants' breath came out in quick little white puffs. One lifted its head and turned it from side to side, but the pheasant was blindfolded with ice and didn't flush.

The boys had not brought clubs, or sacks, or anything but themselves. They stood over the pheasants,

3

turning their own heads, looking at each other, each expecting the other to do something. To pounce on a pheasant, or to yell Bang! Things around them were shining and dripping with icy rain. The barbed-wire fence. The fence posts. The broken stems of grass. Even the grass seeds. The grass seeds looked like little yolks inside gelatin whites. And the pheasants looked like unborn birds glazed in egg white. Ice was hardening on the boys' caps and coats. Soon they would be covered with ice too.

Then one of the boys said, Shh. He was taking off his coat, the thin layer of ice splintering in flakes as he pulled his arms from the sleeves. But the inside of the coat was dry and warm. He covered two of the crouching pheasants with his coat, rounding the back of it over them like a shell. The other boys did the same. They covered all the helpless pheasants. The small gray hens and the larger brown cocks. Now the boys felt the rain soaking through their shirts and freezing. They ran across the slippery fields, unsure of their footing, the ice clinging to their skin as they made their way toward the blurry lights of the house.

# THE FIRST-CALF HEIFER

There was a young heifer that was trying to have her first calf. She lay in the barn tossing her head, heaving, and stiffening her legs, but nothing came out.

The boys stood behind her watching for the front hooves to appear, the tongue between them, and then the nostrils. They had helped lots of calves come into the world before, taking hold of the front feet and pulling when the cow heaved, one time helping with the block-and-tackle when one was taking too long.

But this one was different. There were no feet showing to take hold of or tie on to. When the heifer pushed hard, they could see part of the calf—a black and white Holstein—but no front feet. They couldn't tell for sure what part of the calf was showing through the heifer's small opening.

After a few hours the men were there trying to figure out what to do. One man with small hands worked his arm in when the heifer wasn't pushing. He couldn't figure it out. Things were twisted around and none of the parts were the way they should be for a calf to be born. One hoof was pointed up against the spine, and the man with small hands couldn't move it.

Pretty soon it looked as if the heifer was going to die. She quit trying and lay there waiting for the men to do something.

This calf doesn't want to be born! shouted the man with small hands, and he pulled as hard as he could at the wedged parts. Then he went in with his jackknife and started cutting parts of the calf off and pulling them out.

We're going to have two dead ones if I don't get this out of there, he said. He hurried with his jackknife, cutting off parts that were stuck, pulling them out and putting them into a feed sack that the other men had brought. When all the stuck parts were cut off, what was left slipped out like an egg yolk. The men put this into the sack too. As soon as the heifer looked all right, the men went to the house for coffee.

The boys stayed with the heifer awhile, waiting for the afterbirth to come. But instead, the heifer heaved once and the head of another calf appeared. The boys grabbed its front legs and pulled. This calf came out so fast that the two boys fell over backwards and the calf landed on their laps. The boys laughed to see a calf that was not all cut up into pieces. They rubbed the new calf with straw and let it suck their fingers. It was a healthy calf, and they led it to the heifer's teats. The calf took hold right away. It was hungry from waiting all this time to get out.

When the new calf had drunk its fill, the boys decided to play a joke on the men. They carried the calf outside and called, Come look! Come look! One of the boys had emptied the sack behind the barn so he was holding a bloody empty sack for the men to see.

When the men ran out to see what was happening, one of the boys said, We decided to put the calf back together!

He put the new calf down and it walked straight toward the men.

# BETCHA DON'T DARE

It was risky to dare this one boy because he'd do anything.

Betcha don't dare hang by your heels from the top of the windmill.

He did that, no questions asked. He did it for so long his face turned blue and the other boys screamed at him to please stop.

Betcha don't dare stuff that whole hamburger in your mouth at one time.

He stuffed the whole thing in, onions, pickles, and all. So much hamburger stuffed up in his cheeks made his eyes water, but he reached for another and was going to stuff that in too before one of the other boys said, No, don't, you'll choke.

Betcha don't dare eat a live earthworm.

He took a big one and didn't just swallow it quick like bad medicine. He sucked it in slow like a long strand of live spaghetti until some of the boys were gagging on the words they dared him with.

Then one big boy—and he must have thought about this dare for a long time, because he made sure lots of other boys were around—he said, Betcha don't dare sit on your knees and get a drink of milk from that cow without using your hands. Just your mouth. Betcha don't dare. And you gotta swallow some of it.

It was an old tame cow that was locked in a stanchion and chewing her cud. She was so tame she probably wouldn't have kicked at a rattlesnake, let alone a boy on his knees with his mouth open.

The boy looked at the cow and didn't say anything. Something about this dare made him think for a while. Then he took a deep breath, got down on his knees, and did just what they said, down on his knees, using nothing but his mouth to get at the milk.

The cow turned her head in the stanchion and looked back. She probably had never felt anything like this before. But she didn't kick.

The boy stood up with his cheeks bulging with milk.

Swallow! yelled one boy.

He took a big swallow, then spit the rest of the warm cow milk at the boy who said that.

How did it taste, huh? How did it taste? teased another boy.

Same as always, he said. No different.

# SPRING GRASS

In the spring when the cows were turned out to pasture and ate the new grass, the milk tasted different. That isn't all. The spring grass made their bowels loose.

This was no problem so long as the cows were in the pasture. But when they were in the stanchions, it could be dangerous for someone walking behind them.

One of the boys walked behind a cow one time with a bucket of milk just when the cow coughed. It was like someone slapping him across the face when that cow's loose bowels hit him. And it got all over his clothes and into the bucket of milk he was carrying.

The other boys heard the splattering, and when they saw him, they pointed and laughed. So, to show that he wasn't a sissy, he wiped himself off and then poured that bucket of milk through the strainer right into the big can with the other milk.

This surprised the other boys, and one said, Won't that give us a bad rating with the creamery?

I don't care, said the boy who had been slapped in the face.

The creamery report was a strip of paper with a little circle of cloth that showed how clean or dirty the milk had been, and underneath the cloth was the grade for the week. The white circle on the next report was a little bit cloudy, but the grade said AVERAGE.

That made all the boys laugh.

What do you think happened to that green milk?

One guessed that an old man was putting it in his tea. Another guessed that it had been made into green cheese. But the guess they liked the most was that it had been made into ice cream and shipped to the city.

The boys sat in a circle laughing for hours about all those city kids who were eating that spring grass ice cream and laughing about farm kids who smelled like manure.

# BIG BULL

He was an ordinary Hereford calf when he was born. But friendlier than most. The boys liked him right away and spent more time brushing and playing with him than the other calves.

When the boys walked into the barn, they called, Here, Little Bull, and the animal ran up to them, put his wet nose to their faces, and tried to lick their ears. The boys tickled and wrestled him until he was tired of playing. Then they rubbed his white head and fed him from their hands. He grew very fast. Soon he was big enough to go out into the cattle yard, where the boys rode him bareback from one fence to another. But one day, after Little Bull had playfully thrown one of them off his back, he turned with his head down and pawed the dirt. Maybe Little Bull was still playing. Maybe he was getting mean. That was the day the boys changed Little Bull's name to Bull.

The boys knew the men would sell Bull if they thought he was getting mean. They made sure Bull would stay tame by making a mixture of cracked corn and molasses. Anytime he got a little bit wild, the boys brought the bucket. That good feed always made him happy and friendly.

But it also made him bigger. Much bigger. Soon

he was big enough to breed cows, and the men talked about what a fine bull he was. They figured calves from this fine big bull would be hearty, gentle, and strong. The boys kept playing with him, and feeding him to keep him tame. He only walked when they rode him bareback now, but he still liked the attention. It wasn't long before Bull was fat. When he got his forefeet up on a cow, her back bent like a cherry tree with too many boys on the sack swing. The time came when he was so fat that he could hardly get his chin up on a cow's back, let alone his forelegs. He wagged his tail when the boys approached, but he didn't seem to be able to show his affection in any other way.

That's when the men said, We'll have to sell him. He's so fat he's useless as tits on a boar.

But that wasn't the end of the story for Big Bull. When the stock truck came to get him, he was too big to fit through the chute onto the truck.

The boys thought they and Big Bull might be lucky after all, but the men were very clever that day and thought of a way to put a hay sling around Big Bull's stomach to hoist him high enough for the truck to drive under. The hay sling was just three heavy strands of rope that came together to a ring on each end, like a hammock. Hay was stacked on the sling, and a rope came down from the hoisting beam that stuck out from the top of the barn over the big hay door. And that's how horses pulled big loads of hay up into the haymow.

So the men had the boys lead Big Bull out to the barn with their bucket of cracked corn and molasses. But what the men didn't know is that when the ropes tightened on Big Bull's stomach, he would let out a real loud bellow. Which scared the horses and sent them on a runaway. Which sent Big Bull shooting forty feet straight up like a big yo-yo on a string. The men got the horses stopped, but only after Big Bull was dangling in the middle of the barn, thirty feet above the haymow floor. There was no way to pull Big Bull back out of the barn, since the only rope attached to the hay sling was the trip rope. The men backed the horses up, easing Big Bull down into the haymow. The only way out now was through the little openings in the haymow floor at the tops of the ladders people used to climb up there.

The truck driver went home, promising not to tell anyone. The men closed the big hay door and put the horses away. The boys brought Big Bull a bucket of cracked corn and molasses to make him feel good. In a few minutes everything looked normal. From the outside.

We'll butcher him up there, said one of the men, and nobody will have to know about this.

But one of the boys said, Why don't we just tell people that Big Bull climbed up the haymow?

At first the men said no, but then they looked at one another, grinned, and started laughing. And laughed some more when they thought of the looks on people's faces.

So the men and boys went to the sale barn, where everyone was standing around talking. You know that big bull we got? Well, that critter clumb right up the haymow.

Of course, no one believed this story. Then the men started taking bets, and that got people coming over in a hurry. The boys pulled out some of Big Bull's hair and stuck it to the boards at the top of one of the ladders going up the haymow to make it look like that was the opening Big Bull squeezed through. They loosened a couple of ladder rungs to make it look as if the ladder almost gave way on him as he climbed up.

In a few days people were coming from all over the county to see the big bull that climbed up the haymow. The story made the local newspaper, then Ripley's "Believe It or Not!" Some families brought picnic baskets and made their visit to see Big Bull into an outing.

Big Bull just sat there calmly in the middle of the haymow. He didn't move much, but he looked happier than ever with all this attention—all those people coming to feed and pet and admire him. It was no wonder. He always was a friendly one.

# BLOATING

# AND ITS REMEDIES

One night the cows broke through the fence and got into the alfalfa field. In the morning they were lying in the field bloated. Their stomachs were big mounds, and the hair on their sides looked like grass on a steep hill.

The neighbors came with their remedies. One of them had a sharpened metal tube that he stuck into the paunch to let the air out. Another had a small hose covered with grease that he inserted into the anus. Another had a mixture of soda and soap he made the sick cows swallow.

After watching the men work on the bloated cows for a while, the boys wanted to help. But the men would only let the boys work on a cow they'd already given up for dead. One boy pulled the tail. Another pulled the tongue. The others leaped onto the swollen body and fought for a place on top. Jumped on it. Kicked.

The men pointed and laughed at the boys' foolish efforts. But then one cow exploded, belching and farting and coming back to life in gusts of hot alfalfa fumes. Lurched to its feet, bucked, and threw one of the boys into the air. Then it stood there shaking, looking mixed up, and let the boys stroke its back and rub its ears.

The boys and the cow stood there awhile, looking at each other. The boys almost cried at the sight of this resurrection. Then the men told them to go to the house and wash so they wouldn't smell of it in school.

# CATCHING PIGEONS

Somebody was buying pigeons for forty cents apiece. Why would anyone pay that much for a stupid pigeon? the men asked. Nobody knew for sure, but somebody said something about rich Texans wanting live pigeons instead of clay ones for their skeet shoots.

The boys didn't care. Forty cents was twice what they got for a pair of pocket gopher feet, and catching pigeons would be more fun than trapping pocket gophers.

There must be twenty dollars' worth in our haymow, said the oldest boy. And think of all the neighbors' barns.

What if we run out of pigeons before we're rich? asked another boy. It was a good question, so the boys decided to leave a few pigeons here and there as breeders so they could have a regular income forever.

They found some airy gunnysacks that the pigeons would be able to breathe through and got to work right away.

Some boys crawled along the rope that was strung across the top of the barn for pulling hay into the haymow. This way they could shimmy along just below the roof and trap some of the pigeons in the cupola and catch any that landed on the rope.

The plan worked fine until the boys on the rope started catching pigeons. The idea was to throw them down to the boys who were standing there with the gunnysacks. But it was too far to throw pigeons. Every time one was almost in the hands of a boy below, it beat its wings and got away.

Finally, one of the boys with a gunnysack yelled, Tie the wings, then flip me the bird!

Flip you the bird? said a boy on the rope.

And that was the end of pigeon catching. The rope jiggled with laughter. Then laughing boys fell down into the hay. Laughing boys from below climbed toward them with the gunnysacks, tried to hold a finger up to them, but laughed so hard they couldn't raise their arms.

One laughing boy said, Think of the money, but this sounded funny.

Look! Even the pigeons are laughing, said another laughing boy, and that was funny.

In a little while all the laughing boys and laughing pigeons had laughed themselves right out of the barn.

The boys never did manage to catch those pigeons. Whenever they talked about it, somebody always told the joke instead. Sometimes they thought this was just as good as having lots of money.

# ROTTEN EGGS

In the summertime some chickens would manage to get into the haymows and lay eggs there. They were trying to hide away so they could brood and have chicks instead of having people steal their eggs to eat them. The boys were supposed to find the hidden nests and get the eggs before the hen got the wrong idea about what was going to happen to her eggs.

But the boys had a plan they thought was better than either the hen's or the grown-ups'. They weren't interested in seeing the hen brood and have chicks, but they weren't all that interested in saving every egg for eating either. There were already more than enough eggs for people to eat. What the boys were interested in was rotten eggs. Really rotten eggs. Ones that were so rotten they'd float, so rotten they'd be lighter than marshmallows. A really good rotten egg felt as if it was all shell but was, the boys knew, a stink grenade of the highest quality. A really good rotten egg could smell up a whole building with a stench so strong that it made the boys' mouths water just to think about it. A good rotten egg was worth more than an old baseball card, better than a rare comic book. It would take first place over a tiger-eye marble.

But getting good rotten eggs took work. They had to move the hen and let her know that the only thing she'd get was a kick if she returned to her nest. Then they had to seal off the booty in a spot that was both hidden from view and close to a hot south wall. Now all they needed was patience. They learned they shouldn't watch too closely. It was like watching water when you want it to boil. Best try to forget about the ripening eggs, even when the temperatures were in the nineties for several days running and progress was likely to be rapid. Just pretend they don't exist. They were like wine the grown-ups put in the cellar. Let them get to their best naturally. A month of hot weather was not too much. And if patience prevailed, the rotten eggs would almost float into their hands like gift-wrapped packets of nauseating fumes.

When they finally had what they were waiting for, the boys would sit around examining the eggs and arguing over which one was likely to have the most wretched stench. Sometimes they'd test one on a pig. A good rotten egg was the only thing they knew of that could make a full-grown pig wince. And there was some pleasure in this. Occasionally they'd throw one at another boy in anger, but to waste something so precious in anger never seemed like much revenge. What they liked best was to stand in a circle, especially in a quiet close place, then take turns hurling the explosive eggs down in the center of themselves so they could gag and reel together in hilarious misery and, later, have something wonderful to tell friends who were not lucky enough to have been there with them.

# THE HERNIA

One game was to kneel down next to the pigs while they were eating at the feed trough, and then to turn your head to the side for a pig's eye view of all the pig heads. Then to slide back a bit for a ground-level view of their bellies rising and falling as they swallowed feed. Doing this was how the boys discovered that one of the pigs had a big problem. What looked like a small bald head hung down from one's belly. It almost touched the ground as the pig ate.

The boys ran to tell the men.

It's like a balloon hanging on its belly! one shouted.

The men weren't impressed.

That happens, one of them said. Hernia. Just don't chase that one. If you do, something sharp might cut through the skin and the pig's guts will pour out.

The boys thought about that for a while and talked about chasing the pig to see if this would really happen. But after the jokes, they decided they would rather fix the pig's hernia. It was clear the men weren't going to do anything. They must have thought that there were so many pigs one bad one wasn't worth bothering with.

The boys waited until the pig was sleeping in the

hog house and then, coming low from all directions so the pig couldn't run between their legs, they jumped it, each doing the job he'd agreed on. They wanted to make sure they got the pig's legs pointing up so it wouldn't have any traction. This they managed. The pig still fought and squealed, but they had it in the same position the men got pigs in for castrating—on its back, legs held tight against its body. They almost had the pig rolled in a ball.

And there sat the ruptured hernia, pink as bubble gum and big as a cantaloupe.

One boy ventured to touch it. The skin was tight, but whatever was inside was soft.

It's guts all right, he said.

They took turns feeling. Then two of them put their palms on it and pressed, trying to force the intestines back into the pig's belly. The pig squealed louder. They pressed harder. But the hernia was like a balloon. When you squeeze the air out in one place, it just moves to another.

In a few minutes their arms grew tired and they had to let the pig go. The hernia blew right back up to the size of a little bald head.

They watched the pig after that, the hernia growing a little more each week. The pig always ran off when it saw the boys coming, but they didn't try to catch it again. No matter what happened to the pig, at least they'd had their hands on it. Even if the worst happened, they'd felt the problem with their own hands. That was more than the men could say.

# DANCING WITH CHICKENS

You didn't have to be very smart to know how dumb chickens were. When they were babies, they'd peck each other to death if given half a chance. When they got a little older, they'd smother one another in the corner of the chicken coop if some little thing scared them—a fire-cracker, say, or a good whistle. A weasel could look cross-eyed at a chicken and belly right up to it and have it by the throat before its little bird brain told it anything was wrong. Chickens were so dumb that one would run in front of a car and then squat like it was nesting just when the tire got there. They were so dumb they'd lay the same egg twice if they had their backs to the wind. At least, that's what the boys heard.

What most people didn't know is that chickens could dance. The boys thought this might have something to do with how stupid they were, though they actually seemed to have a knack for it. The boys didn't bring music to dance with chickens, just a little rhythm, a little clapping of hands and shuffling of feet. Not so much that it would scare the chickens into piling in a corner and killing themselves, but hard and loud enough so the chickens' heads would start keeping time. First in little jerky moves while the boys patted their hands, as if the chickens were sniffing the air in the direction of the boys' soft clapping. Then the boys moved their shoulders as they clapped, and the chickens' heads started turning from side to side—at the same time they kept doing their little pecks of the air. Just when everybody was together on this, a whole coop of chickens following the beat, the boys added some foot shuffling, careful not to move so fast that it scared the stupid chickens, never so loud that it sent them squawking into chicken bedlam. After a few seconds of this, one chicken would lift its foot from the straw and then, as if it was too dumb to know what to do with it, put it down again, and then lift the other foot and put it down again, probably because its head was turning and it wasn't sure which direction it would go in if it did try to take a step.

In a while it was a flock of soft jerky dancing, the boys leading the way, keeping it up until they got dizzy—or until they heard someone coming. They didn't want anyone to see them doing this. Dancing with chickens was the only dancing the boys ever did. How would they know for sure that someone watching them wouldn't think the stupid chickens had started all this and they were just following?

# THE SKUNK ROOM

If one smelled this bad, you knew it was either dead or in an awful mood. That's the way it was with a skunk.

When the smell hit them, the boys first looked down the gravel road to see if one had been smeared by a truck. When all they saw was the shimmer of heat waves on gravel, they followed their noses back to the ditch, to the pale milkweeds and thick grass that seemed to ache with skunk smell.

Nothing moved down there. They didn't see any twigs or wood scraps for a skunk to hide under, not even a culvert for a scared skunk to run into. The smell kept coming, strong, like a cup of vinegar in their eyes. This skunk was close by.

But what kind of skunk mood could raise a smell like this? This skunk's mood was so sour, maybe angry or sad or lonely, that it had built a whole room of smell around itself and closed the door. The smell just stood there. The boys walked up against it like a wall that smacked them in the face. They stood at the edge of the skunk's room and tried to stare back into the ditch for a clue. There was nothing as easy as black fur and a white stripe down there. There were no windows, no doorknobs, no chinks of fresh air anywhere. This skunk was serious. This skunk was having the last word on the matter, whatever it was.

# WALKING

# HOME FROM SCHOOL

One spring day the boys stopped on their way home from school to drink water from a puddle along the road. They used sheets from their spelling workbooks to make paper cups.

Except one. He knelt down and drank straight from the puddle. This way he could see his face as he drank.

The others looked into their paper cups before they drank. This way they could see if there were any snakes in the water.

The one who drank kneeling down swallowed a snake. He saw its tail in the water between his eyes, but it was too late. The head was already down his throat.

When he stood up, the boys with paper cups said, You swallowed a snake, didn't you!

The boy who swallowed a snake said he hadn't. He said the water tasted good the way he drank it from the puddle.

The other boys teased him and said his eyes looked different. The boy who swallowed the snake knelt down again and looked in the puddle. He saw a snake. Maybe it was another snake. Maybe it was the snake he had swallowed. Maybe he looked that way now. He told the other boys he did not look different.

As they walked home, the boy felt the snake curl up in his stomach and go to sleep.

This will be easy, he thought. For supper, he said he wasn't hungry. He drank one glass of warm milk. The snake woke up and drank the warm milk, then fell asleep again.

When the boy went to bed, he thought that his stomach looked bigger. So he slept on his back with his hands over his stomach to keep the snake warm.

That night his dreams were different from anyone else's.

The next day no one asked him about the snake.

# THE PET RABBIT

An old man was giving away his rabbits. There must have been fifty of them, all brown, almost the color of Hereford cattle, but of different sizes. He had them packed in orange crates in front of the sale barn. The rabbits didn't try to jump or chew their way out. They just sat there, a big lazy lot, generations of them, from big jowly Grandma and Grandpa to all their hopless leftovers. Just sat there, quiet as oranges. In front of the boxes sat a sign—Enuff Is Enuff! Free Rabbits!—though the old man hadn't dotted the *i* or crossed the *t*.

I can't keep up with them anymore, he said. They just multiplied too fast. Wore me out.

The boys wanted one of those brown rabbits, but they didn't want to get worn out the way the old man had been with a rabbit multiplication problem.

So they chose just the big old grandpa buck rabbit. He wouldn't multiply by himself, and he didn't have enough hop left in him to wear anything out but himself. They named him Duke, took him home, and put him in a cage, though a cardboard box would probably have been strong enough to hold him.

For a few days the boys had the fun of fighting over who got to feed and pet Duke. But in a few more days they were fighting over who *had* to feed him. Then came the problem of needing to clean up Duke's droppings and to put fresh straw in the cage—and whose allowance should pay for the feed pellets anyhow? The only entertainment Duke gave in return was his constant gobbling of feed pellets in on one side and dropping them out the other.

Finally, the boys had to admit that their pet rabbit was about as much fun as a wet sock in a lunch bucket. That poor old man at the sale barn! If one rabbit is this boring, how boring fifty must be!

Maybe we could eat him, said the youngest boy, but this suggestion made the other boys gag.

Maybe we could just let him loose, said another, but they all knew the cats would kill him in a minute since, as another one of them said, he's slower than a sitting duck.

The next week the boys brought Duke to the sale barn. The old man was not there with any rabbits. So the boys put up their own sign. Free Rabbit. Guaranteed Good with Kids, they wrote, carefully dotting the i's and crossing the t's.

You'll never get too much of him, they told the first person who stopped to look.

# HOG CALLS

Sometimes the boys got up very early so they could hear the first hog call of the morning. Hog calling was the farmers' way of getting each other's attention and showing who got up first. The pigs didn't have to be told when it was time to eat and usually beat even the earliest hog callers to the feeding troughs.

The boys liked to sit on top of the supply tank so they could hear in all directions. The first hog call always sounded the best. It seemed to come out of nowhere, like a falling star. It was the one that caused goose bumps and made getting up early worthwhile. It was fun to listen to the other hog calls too, but they all sounded like echoes. The farmers who were not first could just as well have gone out there and yelled, Me too, me too. And the latecomers always tried too hard. They knew they'd overslept and tried to make up for it with weird calls. There was also the favorite joke when a farmer got up late: he'd give somebody else's hog call and try to make the neighbors think he was somebody else, but nobody ever got fooled by this. It was just part of the fun.

The men thought it was a good idea for the boys to get out there and listen to the hog calls. Listening was no way to learn how to do something yourself, but it was a good way to learn how the world worked. Sitting out there in the cold for no good reason certainly was a good start. The men figured it was probably the knack for doing something for no good reason that would make good hog callers out of them all.

# DINNER MUSIC

The time for castrating young boars was very noisy. First the young pigs' squealing and pushing as they tried to get away from the men, and then the louder squealing when the testicles were being cut out.

Even though the noise was terrible, the dog always stood by to eat the testicles as the men threw them away. When the castrating was getting started, the boys stayed away because the awful squealing got on their nerves. But they knew the dog was in the hog house eating testicles, and this made them so curious that after a while they'd come and watch.

The dog stood next to the pen waiting for a flying testicle that the men threw to him. He didn't miss. He made it look as easy as somebody who's good at catching popcorn in his mouth.

Later, when the castrating was over and the squealing had stopped, the boys tried to get the dog to catch dog biscuits the way he caught testicles. But the dog missed the dog biscuits most of the time. At first the boys figured it must have been because he wasn't hungry after his good time in the hog house, but then one of the boys shouted Dinner music! and they all started squealing like pigs. The dog looked at them as if they were crazy, but as long as they screamed he didn't miss a biscuit.

# SPONTANEOUS

# COMBUSTION

One night a neighbor's barn caught fire. Hay that had been put up in the haymow too wet had burst into flames in the middle of the night. The farmer woke up when the light of the burning barn shone in his eyes. It was like a dawn that had come too early. And from the wrong direction.

Fire trucks came from four different towns. All of those sirens woke the neighborhood. Everyone dressed quickly and followed the fire trucks and the light of the burning barn. They parked their cars along the road and in the fields near the fire, then ran out to make a big circle around the barn and the fire trucks.

The barn didn't have a chance. The roof was burning and the framework glowed through the flames like a red-hot skeleton. People stood watching and saying What a shame and What a pity. But the owner was screaming and pointing at the corner of the barn. My pigs! he shouted. They're still in there!

Now the crowd could hear the squealing pigs and the noise of their scuffling bodies against the barn wall. No one talked anymore and a few started walking back to their cars. A young fireman ran toward the barn with an ax and another turned a hose on him so he had a suit of splashing water. He chopped at the barn and right away a pig snout poked through. Now the squealing was louder than ever, but the fireman chopped again and ran back toward the fire trucks. The siding splintered and a large black sow came out, followed by a stream of pigs in all sizes and colors. Ten. Twenty. Fifty pigs. The firemen turned the hoses on them. The pigs sizzled and steamed when the water hit them. They stood still and let the firemen spray them. In a few minutes they ran into the crowd.

At first people did not seem to believe it. The pigs were all right. Someone reached over and rubbed ashes from the singed bristles of one pig. Then everyone was reaching for the pigs and petting them. People started laughing and joking. The whole crowd burst out in celebration. It could have been the Fourth of July or the end of a war, the way they were acting. Somebody had popcorn and somebody else had apples and coffee. They gave some to the owner first and then passed it all around. A case of beer came out of somebody's trunk, then a watermelon and three cantaloupes. And the pigs were part of it all, walking right up to people and eating from their hands. Where are the marshmallows? somebody asked, but no one was interested in the fire anymore. It was one big ball of flames and was not going to do anything but burn itself out. The firemen gave up on it too and started to have fun with the pigs and the other people. They pointed their hoses up. The spray came down on the happy crowd of people and pigs. There should have been a picture of it: all those people and pigs looking up together at a rainbow made by water from fire hoses and the light of a burning barn.

# A GOOD DAY

One day the boys were so happy they didn't know what
to do with themselves.

When they saw a chicken hawk circling overhead,
they spun and held out their arms until they fell down,
dizzy and laughing.

When the young pigs squealed while fighting for
a place at the feeding trough, the boys got down on their
knees and bit each other's ears, laughing and skittering
around until they started wearing out the knees of their
overalls.

They painted mud faces on their bare knees, made
them smile by moving their kneecaps, and then fell over
laughing again.

Running through the cool wet grass, they caught
the cows by their tails and were pulled around the pasture so fast that milk squirted from the cows' teats onto
their shoes. They ran until their shoestrings were dripping with fresh milk.

Everyone got tired, and so did the animals. It
was getting late anyhow, and the cows had to be driven
into the milk barn. It was time for the slow, quiet work
to begin. But when the boys finished milking, that old
happy feeling started coming back.

What to do with it?

Nothing around them seemed to be in the same mood. The cows were chewing their cuds and ready to settle down for the night. Sparrows were already ruffling into their nests. The boys' arms felt loose and lazy too, but the happy feeling wouldn't go away, as if the sun just wouldn't set in them.

One boy leaned against a cow, wondering what to do next, when his elbow touched a small lump on the cow's back. It turned out to be one of many little gifts the boys needed to finish off their good day.

Grubs, they called them.

The cow's back was covered with grubs, small worms that got under the skin on a cow's back and made little mounds that you could feel when you rubbed your hand across a cow's back.

The boys checked the other cows. They all had them! Their backs were like branches of huckleberries with more than enough berries for everyone. The boys picked the cows with the bumpiest backs and climbed on to go to work. They put their thumbs down on the little grub mounds and squeezed. Out came first the creamy body oils and then the fat white worm. The grubs looked as if they were well fed on cow's milk.

Look at this! Look at this one! they shouted as they flicked the little grubs through the air, wiped their hands on the cow's back, and pressed on to the next mound, celebrating in this way the end of a good day.

# DAYDREAMS

One by one the boys drifted off into daydreams. In the
middle of the knee-high bean field, giving in to their
three-hour duty of "walking beans" for sunflowers, for
volunteer corn, for milkweed, for cockleburs. For whatever wasn't beans and needed pulling. For whatever
didn't belong in these green rows of soybeans soybeans
soybeans. Each in his own way, they drifted off.

   And while drifting they stooped or bent, pulling
out or breaking off what didn't belong, now when the
sun was more wet than hot and the smells rising from the
field were like the odors from an old bed, flatter or duller
than the smell of soybeans or whatever didn't belong.
Shuffling steadily, they drifted off, moved past duty or
work, past praise or blame, without word or effort,
crossed that line into the blur of trying and not trying,
of doing and not doing, where tedium could be leisure
and boredom contentment.

# FALL

There was a chill in the air. The birds felt it and started to hide out or pull out; the yellow and gray fields seemed to sulk in it with their faces of bent stems and crumbling furrows. Even the squirrels knew it was time for something, busy scratching through fallen leaves for what would have been easier to find under greener conditions. The boys felt surrounded by shades of nothing in particular and felt like they had to do something about it.

But what could you do at a time like this? You could leave whatever fall was trying to be and make caves out of hay bales. Deep dark caves, if you spent enough time at it. You could go right into a big square stack of hay bales and unbuild it any way you felt. You could give a haystack a stomach, then give it big hollow arms. You could give it intestines! You could make tunnels and crossroads and drop-offs. You could make any kind of cave you wanted, if you weren't afraid of a little work and didn't bother with the weather. And you could seal off all the light with handfuls of hay wedged between bales, and you could hide the cave entrance with another bale. From the outside, all the world would see was a big old block of hay bales waiting to get heavy with winter snows. But you could build caves in there. Then you could slide in and take a world of darkness with you. You could just sit there like bats, not needing any eyes, and have a whole cave to yourselves.

And that's what the boys did.

# ELECTRICITY

The boys remembered the night electricity came to the farm. At least the oldest did, and the others pretended to. Or they'd heard the story so often they thought they remembered it. After a while, it didn't matter who really remembered it and who didn't. They all knew the story.

It was the night the big switch was thrown somewhere at some big dam. This was long after the electrician had spent weeks wiring all the buildings, putting switches on walls where only wallpaper had been, putting a long fluorescent light like the ones they'd seen in town right in the middle of their kitchen ceiling so that the old lantern had to hang on a new hook until the big switch was thrown.

The night of the big switch: that's when all these dead wires and gray light bulbs were supposed to come to life. Could it really work? Could electricity get all the way out here from that big switch at that big dam hundreds of miles away?

A letter had come telling how to get ready for the big night. Five o'clock p.m. on such-and-such a day the big switch would be thrown. Have all switches turned off, the letter said, and turn them on one at a time. As if the big dam couldn't stand to have all of its electricity sucked out at once. Which made sense to the boys. Cows kicked if you tried to milk all four teats at once. And a horse would take more easily to four riders if they didn't all get on at once. Imagine a chicken laying ten eggs in one shot. It made sense.

So the night of the big switch they sat around the kitchen table waiting, switches turned off. Waiting for five o'clock. Then they saw it happen—a light on the horizon where there hadn't been a light before. Then a light in the neighbor's window, about a half-mile away. Then lights popping on everywhere. It looked as if the whole world was covered with fireflies. The new light was not the yellow light of lanterns but the white clear light of electricity. Light clear as water from the big dam, wherever it was.

One of the boys flicked the kitchen switch. And it happened right there. The big switch worked, even here. It was as if the ceiling opened with light. A fluttering fluorescent angel of light. A splash, a woof, a clatter of light. And in one second there was more light in that kitchen than had ever been there. Light brighter than high noon on the Fourth of July. They looked at each other in this new light—every freckle, every smudge, every stringy hair, every ring around the collar clearer than ever. Then they looked around the room—the cupboards, the wainscoting, the wallpaper, the ceiling where the old lantern dangled like a hanged man.

And out of the throat of one of the horrified light-stricken grown-ups came the words, My goodness! Look how dirty this place is!

So the first night of that great fluorescent light

they spent washing the walls. Every one of them. Every inch.

That was the story the boys knew. That was the story they would always be able to tell, whether they remembered it or not.

# THE HIKE

The boys went for a hike around the section. Four miles. They packed a lunch in an empty gallon syrup can and set off at noon. They knew they'd be doing some things along the way—watching for wild strawberries, checking out a couple creeks, crawling through some culverts, maybe chase a few calves, make a visit to their favorite apple orchards, tease a few geese if they came toward the road, that sort of thing—but they figured they'd be done by four o'clock. Plenty early for afternoon chores, anyhow, so no one would complain that they'd been gone too long.

You can't plan for blisters on your heels or sunburn on the spot where your shirt sleeves are too short. You can't plan on bumblebees in the roadside ditches, or for twisted ankles from jumping off a little bridge. No one expects barbed-wire cuts or getting caught in somebody's apple tree, or getting nipped by a goose that has a worse bite than a rat terrier. And who'd expect to get bawled out for using a few leaves of corn for toilet paper, or that there'd be leeches in the neighbor's creek? And what's wrong with putting a seed corn sign at the edge of an alfalfa field as a joke? And how much trouble could it have been for people to find their mail when it had been switched to a neighbor's mailbox that was only a half-mile away? And if somebody's bull is mean, why not tease him a little by waving a shirt to show him he shouldn't be so serious about things? And isn't it a good idea to throw some weeds over the telephone wires so birds can eat without worrying about lurking cats? And who would ever think there'd be a problem with filling one end of a culvert with stones so that the next rabbit that thought it could run in one side and out the other would have another guess coming? And so what if there's an apple stuck in the end of the muffler on somebody's tractor—it would just blow out when the tractor started. And just what good do the glass insulators on telephone poles do anyway?

When the boys set off, they had in mind just your standard hike around the section. How were they to know it would be six o'clock before they were back, that they'd be all scratched up, bitten, stung, tired, hungry, let alone practically crippled, and screamed at like some kind of menace to the community? And that so many people for miles around would waste their own time yelling across fences and fields and using what was left of their telephones just to ask each other, Where are they now and what are they up to?

# PART II

THE YOUNGEST BOY

# THE YOUNGEST BOY

It was not easy being the youngest boy. Being the last one in the race to the house for supper. Being the one who held the wrenches while the others fixed the bicycle. Being the one no one would believe when everybody else was lying. And the one who could not back his anger with muscle.

But there was an advantage to being small. Some nights, very late, when he wanted the world to himself, he slipped out of bed with such small noises that no one heard. And he moved through the house making sounds that the rats or wind might make. Then he waited until the wind changed enough to move the metal fan on the windmill so it squeaked. At the same time, he opened the screen door and the two squeaks went together and he was outside. Here there were always some animal sounds, and it was easy to fit them in with the sounds of his walking and overall legs rubbing together. Steers rubbing against wooden fences because the grubs in their backs did not sleep at night. Or sick pigs that had swallowed wire plodding to the drinking trough to quench the burning in their stomachs. Even birds and chickens with their little fluttering pains. With his flashlight still turned off, he went down to the barn and the door with new hinges that didn't squeak. Inside, he turned on the flashlight and shone it in the faces of calves who got up to see what there was to eat, then lay down again. He made up little songs and sang to them. Sometimes the songs were silly, sometimes they were mean. The calves hardly listened, but they learned not to complain, and not to expect anything either.

# THINKING ABOUT THE SNOW

Why was no one afraid of the snow? When a dark cloud hung low in the southwest in the summer and the air grew still and heavy, people looked at each other as if to ask, Is your soul ready for the hereafter? Or when the spring thaw came too quickly and the creeks rose with large tables of ice turning and overturning in the current, people looked around for the highest ground as if closeness to the sky, not the earth, might save them. And hailstorms, or wind gusts that took with them more than their fair share of leaves—these scared people.

But snow—once the winds had calmed down and no one was afraid of walking blindly in circles—snow could rise in banks as high as telephone poles, could block doorways or form elephant-sized drifts wherever it wanted, and it still made almost everyone but the mailman smile, even if it meant an extra hour or two of work shoveling paths through it.

The youngest boy sat inside the house looking out at the massive whiteness, wondering if he was the only person on earth it made uncomfortable. It's so big, he thought, it looks like it's trying to take over the whole world. Once he even dared to ask why no one was afraid of the snow, but he was made fun of and didn't ask again. He would join the other boys in the newly fallen snow only when he had to, and he usually waited until someone else had made safe paths through it. Then he might go out, but only after putting on extra layers of clothing while no one was watching. If he was given half a chance, he'd stay inside. Sometimes he sat alone near a window, rubbing his small hands, blowing gently on them, pretending they were flowers.

# EYE TO EYE

The boys liked to watch pigs being born. Drying them off in the straw. Putting them next to the sow's teats. Watching them discover the little world of the farrowing pen. But after a while the boys would get tired of this and go off to do something else.

Except for the youngest boy. He liked to stick around by himself. When the other boys left, he leaned over and put his face down close to the sow. Now that there was no one there to laugh at him. This way he could hear the pig coming and when it was born his face was right over the newborn. He quickly put his eye over the eye of the little pig. When it opened its eye, the first thing it saw was the boy's eye, only an inch or two away from its own.

The boy stared into the pig's eye and the pig stared into the boy's. What the boy liked to see was the expression on the pig's face. It was a look of surprise. But not a big surprise. Not the startled look of seeing something you didn't expect to see—like a ghost or a creature from Mars. More like the look of somebody waking up in the backseat of a car who doesn't realize how far he's gone since he fell asleep. The look that says, Oh, I didn't know we'd gone this far, but okay.

Then the boy lifted his head so the pig could notice everything else. The pig knew what to do. Stand up, breathe, look around for a nipple. The boy didn't try to keep the pig from its business. He knew they both had their own worlds to live in. That didn't change the fact that for a few seconds they had been somewhere that nobody else would ever have to know about.

# SPRING

The youngest boy didn't know what to make of spring smells. The smells were strange and everywhere, oozing from pores of tree or fence post, from barn or cat. Spring smells from bird nests, from fading sheets of snow that let out sod and mulch.

Sounds he understood—ice crackling a warning in roadside ditches when he skidded across them, crows chattering and mating in box elder trees. He knew the touch of spring too, the slide and fall of melting mud, cold slush on his ankles, or the pulse of spring's warm gusts—these he understood as clearly as the young calves' urge when loosened from indoor pens to dance in the slippery fields.

But for the youngest boy spring really started in the air, coming to him not as clean, fresh-air smells but as thick, rich smells that were neither sweet nor foul. Breathing the full odors of spring left the boy teetering, unsure of where he was in the picture he saw around him. It was like a big body close to him, sweating, but he couldn't see or touch it. Something more is coming, he felt, something more than I am ready for or know what to do with.

# HEAD LICE

It was more than an itch, it was head lice.

Why did I get them and nobody else? asked the youngest boy. It's not fair.

But the youngest boy's troubles had just begun. Get away from us! said the older boys. Get your clothes out of our room! Don't use our combs! Don't touch our toothbrushes!

But when the youngest boy was having his head treated with tar soap, the older boys got curious. The fine-tooth comb raked the dead lice from his hair. They stacked up on the table like little vegetables from the first garden pickings. Then, after the rinsing, the work on the nits began, sliding the little white eggs off the hair between fingernails.

I see one! one of the older boys said, and reached for the hair to pull the nit off between his fingernails.

There's another one! said another boy.

Getting all the nits was a big job, so one of the grown-ups made popcorn while the boys worked on the nits. They would have a little celebration when the work was done. The boys made the work more interesting by counting to see who could pick the most nits. Now, instead of crawling with lice, the youngest boy's head was crawling with hands. Everybody was talking at once. His hair was like a field of oats in July, filled with busy harvesters.

# THE THROW-UP PAN

One winter the boys all got the flu at the same time. The headaches and fever and nausea were bad enough, but the worst thing was that there was only one throw-up pan to go around. During the day this was no problem—they put it in the middle of the room, and whoever needed it could walk or crawl over to it. But at night in the dark was different—someone might wake up needing it right away and not be able to find it in time.

So the boys fought over who got to sleep with the throw-up pan next to his pillow. When they drew straws for it, somebody would always wait until the others were asleep and then sneak over and get it to put by his own pillow.

The oldest boy had an idea. Since it was a metal pan, they could punch little holes in the rim. This way they all could tie a string to it. The throw-up pan could stay in the middle of the room and each one could have the end of his string next to his pillow to pull if he needed to throw up in a hurry.

This method worked fine. Most of the boys tied their favorite toy to their end of the string so it would be easy to find in the dark. But the youngest boy tied his string to a loose tooth. He figured this way it would be easy to find his string if he needed the pan, and if someone else needed it he would get rid of the loose tooth while asleep. Since the older boys no longer had baby teeth, they could not use the youngest boy's idea, but they still gave him credit. Why not? During a bad time like that, anybody's good idea would make things seem a little better for everybody.

# BAT WINGS

On summer nights when the sun was just setting and things were starting to get boring, the men sometimes went outside with their shotguns to shoot bats. On good nights the bats circled and dived for insects over the men's heads. The men swung their guns wildly and took quick shots from the hip. But other times the bats hovered high overhead, giving the men a chance to take careful aim. That was when they found out just how good the bats' radar was, because the bats moved so quickly that the shot still missed them. At those times they seemed to jump in midair, looking more like hummingbirds than bats.

The shotguns were an awfully noisy way not to get bats, and it was the boys who thought of a quiet way you could. Fishing for them. They took some of the men's fly rods and started casting the flies into the sky.

When the hunting isn't good, one boy said to the men, you should try fishing. The men put their guns down to watch. Soon one boy lured a bat by casting a fly rod. The bat dived for the fly and was caught. The boy reeled the bat in from the sky while the men watched, looking surprised, with their quiet guns across their knees.

Then the men wanted to try fishing for bats and sometimes had the same good luck the boys were having.

After they caught a half-dozen bats like this, they noticed that the bats never had the hook in their mouths. It was always stuck in the bats' wings.

If they have such good radar, why don't they catch the fly in their mouths? asked one of the men.

The youngest boy said, Maybe their wing's just like a hand and they have to catch the fly first.

The youngest boy's idea sounded so silly that no one paid him any attention, but years later—at thousands and thousands of dollars' expense—somebody in a laboratory found out that bats really do catch their food in their wings.

# RINGWORM

The boys knew there were three ways to get rid of ring-worm. You could go to a doctor once for some medicine, you could take a piece of cotton batting and dab kerosene on it two or three times, or you could put butter on it and let a dog lick it five or six times a day for a week.

We've got plenty of butter, said the smallest boy when he had ringworm. I might as well put butter on it five or six times a day for a week and let the dog lick it off.

His ringworm covered a round spot from the tip of his chin to his Adam's apple. He buttered this spot, then lay on his back in the lawn with his chin up. The first time he invited the dog to lick the butter off, the dog was leery, sniffing the boy but not daring to lick. It must not have seemed like the right thing to do, like tak-ing a cookie off a picnic table, the sort of thing that usually brought a swat to the ears. But after a few times, the dog understood that it was all right and came run-ning when he saw the boy lie down and raise his chin.

The boy liked ringworm lickings too. In the morning the ringworm was itchy, and the licking took away some of that misery. In the afternoons, after he had gotten sweat on it, the ringworm was sore and the licking wasn't very pleasant. So he worked out a schedule of four lickings in the morning when the itching was bad, and maybe just one or two in the afternoon when it was tender. Mornings also happened to be the time that the hardest work had to be done, and he didn't want to get any more sweat on the ringworm than he had to.

By the fifth day of the lickings, the ringworm was almost gone. It didn't itch in the mornings anymore and it wasn't sore in the afternoons.

It's a little bit better, he said. But it might take longer than a week.

In the meantime, the boy put more and more butter on the ringworm and the dog licked slower and slower, each doing what was possible to make the cure last as long as they could.

# THE INSIDE RATS

During the day, when the boys saw a rat near the corn-crib or barn or eating from a pig trough, it was as if a match had been struck inside them. They dropped whatever toys they were playing with and ran for pitchforks or sticks, hot for the kill.

But at night the boys sometimes lay awake listening to rats run through the attic and walls. The ones that made it that far up in the house were usually lost and ran wildly back and forth, trying to find a way out. The boys knew one place near the ceiling where there was a hole. When a lost rat ran over that spot, it fell between the wall studs down to the floor, right there in their room with nothing but the thin wall separating them. Then the boys had the fun of hearing the rat scramble around trying to climb back up the plaster boards. When they put their hands on the wall, they could feel the rat's claws scratching on the other side. They could tell how far up the rat was, and when they slapped that spot, the rat fell to the floor to try again.

Once, instead of slapping the spot the rat was trying to climb back up to, the youngest boy put his palm on the wall to feel where the rat was scratching. The rat's clawing tickled his fingertips and the boy scratched back. The rat must have liked this, because it tickled one return scratch, then calmly climbed up its side of the wall and tiptoed through the attic back to wherever it came from.

# SOME THEORIES

# ON RAT TAILS

One thing the boys noticed about cats and rats was that when a cat ate a rat, it always left the tail.

So why didn't cats eat the rats' tails?

I know! said one boy. They leave it for the rat-tail fairy, who puts out a bowl of milk for it!

No, stupid, said the oldest boy. Then you'd find bowls of milk instead of rat tails!

I know, said another boy. They leave it there so it will grow back another rat for them to eat!

No, stupid, said the oldest boy. Then you'd see all these rat tails with only half-grown rats on them!

I know, said the littlest boy. The cats use the rat tails for toothpicks.

The oldest boy could not think of any reason why this might not be so. But he still said, Have you ever seen a cat pick its teeth with a rat's tail?

No, said the littlest boy, but have you ever seen a cat with dirty teeth?

The boys went out and checked some cats' teeth. They were clean.

I always knew toothbrushes were humbug, said the oldest boy, who always wanted to have the last word.

# BOX-ELDER BUGS

How many box-elder bugs do you think there are crawling on this tree?

The boy who asked this flicked dozens of the harmless little orange and black creatures to the ground.

It was a silly question. Like asking how many dandelions there are in the pasture after a rainstorm. It would have been smarter to ask, What with all these box-elder bugs, how long do you think it will be before somebody gets one in his mouth?

That would have been a question worth thinking about, because anybody with any sense would know that anything as small and plentiful would have to make its way into somebody's mouth sooner or later.

All the boys had gotten their fair share of little creatures in their mouths already. They all knew the taste of a gnat or, for that matter, a grasshopper—and even in a dry year there weren't half as many grasshoppers as box-elder bugs. Who's going to taste one first? would have been a sensible question.

It felt a little bit like an unripe grain of oats in the corner of the youngest boy's mouth. Like an unripe grain of oats with the soft, wingy husks still on it. How it got there while he was walking under a box-elder tree wasn't a question he thought to ask at the moment. It felt so much like an unripe grain of oats that he coaxed it into his mouth, moving it with his tongue to the front of his eyeteeth, where he ground it up like an almost-crunchy grain of oats.

The youngest boy was old enough to know that new tastes in the mouth have a way of wanting to be an old taste with a new twist. Like milk that is going sour or bread that is getting mold on it. Or like an unripe grain of oats with milkweed juice on it, he figured.

It was not until he had given the gooey box-elder bug a chance to smear itself on all the taste buds that he gave up and spit the problem into his palm. Even given its sad condition, the youngest boy could spot its little black head, the spindly legs, even a few orange dots on the free-floating feather-shaped wings.

This was one of those moments he decided to keep to himself. Nothing to brag about. Nothing worth telling to the older boys. The only good he thought could come of this would be if someday he saw a twitch on someone's face at the sight of box-elder bugs, that little signal that says, I know, I've been there too. Only then would he say anything. Maybe something like, Sure are a lot of them, aren't there? Wonder what they taste like.

# THE DANDELION

One summer day the boy walked out into the pasture to
be alone. The land was flat, but he knew a place where
maybe many years ago someone had taken out a big rock,
and now there was a little dent in the grass, big enough
to lie down in and not be seen. This is where he went,
even though he knew it was where everybody went who
wanted to hide.

He lay down on his back and looked straight up
into the sky. Now and then he saw an insect fly over, and
after a while he saw a chicken hawk making a big circle
above him, so high it must have been cruising the air for
fun, not looking for field mice or dead chickens. He heard
animals cough a long distance away. He heard wind in
the grass and the faint sound of a screen door closing.
He heard a tractor start and then stop again. He turned
on his side and closed his eyes. He could smell the grass,
and when he put his face down to the earth he could smell
something deeper than the grass, a sweet lemony smell at
the very roots of the pasture. He felt the sun warm his
face and turned toward it again. When he opened his
eyes, he saw a dandelion a few inches away, its yellow
more yellow than he had ever seen. And as he stared at
this silly meadow weed, he saw it breathe, its golden face

like a tiny chest taking in and letting out—the dandelion was breathing!

He stood up, faced the direction of the farm buildings and the chores that were probably waiting for him. He had been alone too long. He had almost gone too far with this. He took off, running back toward the farm buildings like someone who just can't wait to see everybody.

# CORNCOBS

# AND PEACH TISSUES

During the summer the boys had to use the outhouse. It was a rule. No sense using all that water for flushing and no sense tracking up the house when the weather is nice enough to use the outhouse.

The boys didn't mind using the outhouse. Except for the corncobs. After a while the corncobs didn't bother them, but the boys were always glad when peaches arrived at the grocery stores in town. They didn't like peaches very much, but they liked the soft tissue paper that peaches were packed in. When the peaches were unpacked, the soft paper was put in the outhouse and could be used instead of corncobs.

When the peach tissues were used up, it was back to corncobs. Just when the boys were getting used to the soft tissues! For a few weeks their tender skin got sore from the corncobs. But then they would get used to scratchy cobs and weren't bothered by them very much.

The corncobs and tissues got the boys to talking seriously about what might be learned from all this.

Having things bad is not so bad as long as you don't know how good things can be, said one.

Yes, but having things good after having things bad is even better than having things good when they've been good all the time, said another.

But I think even though having things bad after having them good is worse than not knowing how good things can be, it's still better to have some good with the bad than not to have any good at all, said the oldest boy.

But it isn't exactly six of one and half-dozen of the other, said the youngest boy. There are more corncobs than peach tissues in the world, that's for sure.

# SWIMMING

The boy was dropped off at the sand pit, which was the swimming pool around there. Everyone trusted him that he could be there by himself, that he wouldn't go trying to swim beyond the rope.

They were right. He knew how much he couldn't swim. He dog-paddled along just inside the rope where his toes could still touch bottom but in water deep enough that people wouldn't be able to see his legs and tell that he wasn't really swimming.

It was when he saw the girl on the beach towel that he started feeling foolish, saw her watching him, and saw how he must look to her, what with his big arms brown to the elbows and then going on like a couple of white pillars to his shoulders. She had already seen his white legs coming in. She knew that his feet could touch bottom inside the ropes. She knew he wasn't swimming.

Who gave her that tan face? Who taught her to smile as if nothing bad could ever happen to her?

When she stood up, she looked like something from the water returning home, and she did return home, like an eel, entered the water so smoothly she was like a ribbon and her hair followed her like smaller ribbons.

The boy stood up to admit he wasn't swimming, watched her ease by and turn onto her back, smiling at him. She wasn't making fun. She wasn't teaching. She was swimming.

# SPECS

It was hard having thick glasses if you lived on a farm, but the youngest boy treated Specs like everyone else. Except he called him Specs, which was all right with Specs so long as the youngest boy wasn't teasing and so long as he didn't call him that in front of grown-ups, who didn't understand that it was all right.

But one day the youngest boy was in town with Specs when a stranger, a town boy, called Specs Four Eyes.

Don't call my friend Four Eyes, said the youngest boy.

Four Eyes Four Eyes Four Eyes Four Eyes, said the town boy and shoved the youngest boy so hard he fell to the ground.

I'm not afraid of you, said the youngest boy and stood up. Don't call my friend Four Eyes.

Now the town boy punched the youngest boy in the face, a quick, easy punch as if he were punching air for fun. But the easy punch made an easy hit. One of the youngest boy's long front teeth sliced a neat hole in his lip, and he bled. He bled a lot. Blood all over his mouth and chin. Then over both hands and sleeves when he wiped his mouth. He bled like a stuck pig, but when he saw how much the blood scared the town boy he started blowing blood bubbles and acting as if he couldn't catch his breath. The blood kept coming and dripped down on his shirt. There was power in this blood. He leaned forward and let blood drip on the tops of his white tennis shoes. He didn't let any of it get away. The town boy squirmed like a snake with a horse on its tail. The youngest boy hoarded blood all over himself.

Specs just stood there owl-eyed.

It was an accident, the town boy said. He shivered and caught his breath, as if he were bleeding too. What are you guys's names? he said.

But all that blood wailed a message across town. Grown-ups came running from stores and jumping out of cars. They gave the bleeding boy a lot of attention, then called the town boy a big bully, the worst they'd ever seen, and didn't bother to ask Specs if he had seen what happened. But they had their grown-up say in the matter: What kind of boy are you anyhow, hitting somebody in the face? Are you some kind of maniac? Who are your parents anyhow? Wait until they hear about this. Don't you ever come near these boys again.

The boys listened but weren't surprised when they all saw each other in town again the next week. The three of them looked at each other from different sides of the street, the way stray dogs do. Specs and the youngest boy figured that if they spoke first, there might be another fight. If the town boy talked first, there might not be. It was one of those times when a little silence seemed like the best peace talk.

The town boy came to their side of the street. Are you all right? he said. It was something he could say to sound tough and nice at the same time.

Sure, they said. Did you get in any more trouble? They knew their power too—the whole world had been on their side.

And so the three of them got together. The only thing the town boy had in his fist now was some corn candy. He gave some to Specs first, holding it close to his face. The three walked off to one of the side streets where people wouldn't notice them. They told each other their names, compared scars they'd gotten from various fights and accidents, and made a few secret agreements for the future.

# THE INSURANCE ADJUSTOR

A few weeks after the hailstorm, the insurance adjustor came around.

You want to learn something, boy? You just come with me to see how these slickers operate. They wait a while hoping we'll be thankful they show up. They'll try to get us to sign anything.

The youngest boy followed the man out to meet the insurance adjustor next to the cornfield. The only thing the boy knew was that you don't want to smile in front of the insurance adjustor. You don't want to give him ideas that anything was all right.

No two fields are alike, was the first thing the adjustor said. Storms are funny that way.

He took out his paper and pen and started counting holes in the corn leaves.

Nothing funny about this storm, said the man, who had his own pad of paper along with his own pencil, a big flat carpenter's pencil that made the insurance adjustor's thin pen look like a toy model. Look at the ears, he said to the adjustor. Those hailstones knocked the milk out of half the kernels on some of them ears.

The insurance adjustor peeled back the green husk on an ear. He touched the soft kernels as if they were tender blisters. He smoothed the husk back up over the kernels, and the youngest boy thought he acted like a doctor putting the covers back over a sick person. Then the adjustor wrote something down on his paper with his little pen. The man held his big pencil and watched the insurance adjustor.

How many acres like this? asked the adjustor.

Eighty acres.

Is this the worst?

This is bad enough, said the man.

If there's any worse, I'll look at it too.

No, I guess this is pretty much it, said the man.

The insurance adjustor did some calculating. I figure you've got eighty-eight percent, he said. Twelve percent damage. My company will pay you twelve percent the worth of the average corn crop in this township over the past five years. Is that satisfactory?

What did you give the neighbor? said the man.

Ten percent. Like I said, these storms pick and choose. No two of them alike. Then the adjustor looked out across the field. Exactly eighty acres here?

Uh, just a little off for the railroad track. We say eighty.

Then I'll say eighty, said the adjustor.

There was a lot of silence then as the adjustor filled out some papers and handed them over to be signed. The man started to use his big pencil, but the line he was supposed to sign on was too small. He handed his pad and thick pencil to the boy, then accepted the adjustor's skinny pen to sign the papers. The two men shook hands and the adjustor drove off.

You can't trust anybody anymore, said the man and walked away.

The boy stood there holding the big pencil and pad of paper, not sure what he had learned from all this.

# THE SHOTGUN

The shotgun hung inside on the porch, right over the front door. The old yardstick used for spankings hung over the pantry door. Both were off limits.

When no grown-ups were around, the youngest boy was tempted to get his hands on both of them, but mostly on the shotgun. He'd check out the shotgun first, pulling up a chair to lift the large, heavy thing down. With its walnut stock and dark metal barrel, the shotgun was the most beautiful thing in the house. He'd put it to his shoulder and take aim at the little ring that hung down from the cord on the window blind. He didn't think of killing anything. He thought about the gun, about how lively it could be. He liked the way it could spit fire in the dark when the men were night hunting. He liked the way it jumped when it exploded. He liked the smooth click of the chamber opening and closing, like sharp teeth coming together, teeth as precise as tweezers. He liked the little BB sight on the end of the barrel. He liked the feel and heft of it.

He would hold the shotgun and, after aiming it here and there, draw it close and rub his hand across the length of the barrel, then look down its shiny ringed throat. He rubbed the wooden stock, ran his fingernail along the engraved wheat design. He sniffed it. More than anything he liked the smell of gunmetal and gun-powder and the faint smell in the wood of oil from a man's palms. When it was time to put the shotgun back, he wiped it off with a handkerchief and hung it back on its hooks above the door, and it looked even more beautiful from his having touched it.

Then he wandered into the kitchen before he heard anyone coming. The pantry was where extra cookies might hide, and the yardstick above its door was supposed to warn him not to go in there. He knew the pain of that yardstick. The yardstick hung there guarding the cookies. But the shotgun hung over the door that guarded the whole house. The shotgun was the biggest thing he knew. Holding it for a while made him lose his appetite for a cookie, made cookies seem as flimsy as the silly stick that was supposed to protect them.

# BIRD SONGS

The youngest boy loved the songs of the birds he shot with his BB gun. Near sunset, when the distant barns and silos were like notes against the rose curtain of sky, he went out with his BB gun, following his favorite bird songs. The sparrow to its nest in the hog house cupola, the pigeon cooing under the eaves of the barn, the brown thrasher in the ash tree, the barn swallow on the telephone wire, the robin in the apple tree, the mourning dove on the highest box elder branch, the meadowlark at the top of a thistle.

Hunting for the singing birds was like hunting for the song. The one he liked best was the wren's, though it was the smallest bird and hardest to hit. Whenever he heard its song, often from the deep leafy cover of a weeping willow, he would move very slowly, listening to its sweet sharp song, watching for the quick twitch among leaves. When the wren was his, the warm feathers in his hand, he would hold it toward his lips, study the mystery of its tiny throat, and practice whistling its song.

# THEY ARE LIKE CALVES

One Saturday night the youngest boy slipped off by himself to see what the town boys were doing by the grandstand in the park. They saw him coming. They could tell a farm boy by the big steps he took and by the way he looked around when there was nothing to look at. The boy saw them looking, all turning their heads together like so many young calves in a pasture when a tractor goes by.

He saw a water fountain and headed straight for it, as if getting a drink of water was why he came to the park in the first place. The town boys recognized this tactic and headed for the same water fountain. The boy couldn't change his course without looking foolish, so he hurried up, hoping he'd get there first, take a quick sip, and head back toward the gas station Coke machines, where all the farm boys hung out. But the town boys hurried up too, and beat him to it. So the boy pretended there was a line at the water fountain and stood behind it, waiting his turn. He kept looking around curiously, even though there wasn't a thing to look at.

Some water got splashed on him, so he stepped back a little. The town boys laughed and splashed a little more water on him. They were still like young calves who'd just been turned out and had never felt the slash of a barbed wire or the sting of an electric fence. They were like young calves that had never been lassoed and tied down while their little horns were cut off right above the ears.

Where'd you get *those* shoes? said one of the town boys.

None of your business, he said, and didn't know what he was saying until he heard himself say it.

There were a few pushes and some spitting on the boy's back.

I betcha them thar shoes have shoestrings long enought to tie yer shoes together, I betcha, said the biggest town boy.

Yeah, tie your shoes together and git ouda here, said another.

Nothing wanted to come out of the boy's mouth this time. He knelt down and unlaced his ankle-high work shoes, laced one shoe to the other, and shuffled awkwardly away as the town boys laughed and taunted and spit water on him halfway back to the gas station.

They really are like calves, he thought as he shuffled along. They have no idea what it would be like to have someone chase them with a tractor through snowbanks up to their chins. Or what it would be like to have someone sprinkle pepper on their salt licks. They have no idea what it would feel like to have a BB hit them in the nuts while their backs are turned, maybe while they're grazing, or a pitchfork in their ribs when they didn't stay in line coming into the barn. They have no idea at all.

# THE PONY

He was a small brown Shetland named Beauty. The youngest boy fed him apples, and this would hold off the bucking when he rode. But no one had taught the boy how to train a pony, so he treated Beauty the way he might treat a dog, offering food when he wanted the pony to do something—which was never any more than a short ride around the farmyard. Beauty started training the boy, kicking at him, biting his leg when he mounted. The boy took these punishments as requests and fed Beauty what he wanted. Then Beauty would let him ride for a little ways down the drive, but the rides got shorter and shorter before Beauty would make the next demand—a buck, a bite, a kick, whatever it took to get an apple or teaspoon of sugar.

One day when the boy was busy with something else, maybe forgetting about Beauty because the rides had been reduced to only a few steps, the pony made his way to the oats bin and, wanting to get his way, nudged the door until it opened. Beauty had his fill of oats, ate far more than he needed, far more than was good for him. For a few days he was sick, and then his hooves began to grow. And to grow. Overeating like that had caused the pony to founder, and his hooves grew until they stuck out in front of his heels like wooden *klompen*.

Beauty couldn't kick the boy after that. He would try to bite the boy if he came near, but this rarely happened. What was the point of giving him any apples? The boy couldn't ride Beauty anymore, and he didn't have to get close to watch the struggle for every painful step.

# THE DRIVER

The gravel truck didn't even slow down. The youngest boy heard the *whump whump,* but the dog didn't howl, didn't bark, didn't say anything. The boy had his back to the road, was across the ditch and across the fence, in the pig grass, doing something. He didn't even remember what. Just doing something. Nothing bad. Nothing he would have gotten in trouble for if a grown-up had seen him. *Whump whump* and a cloud of dust and through the dust the yellow dog flat on the gravel road.

When the boy got there, on the middle of the road, he was afraid he wouldn't know what to do. Then he saw the dog's eyes were popped out. That didn't leave any guessing. That didn't leave any room for panic. The eyes said it all: Don't worry, I'm dead. I'm not even a dog anymore.

The boy looked close, looked at those eyes hard, how they were really out there, almost an inch from the sockets. And a little drool of blood from the mouth, like a small apron under the dog's nose. He looked hard at it all, then nudged the stomach with his toe, bent down, lifted a hind leg, and dropped it. He kicked the dog once. Nothing more.

And then the grief.

Days later, when he wasn't crying, when the

shocks in his chest didn't come at him anymore when he least expected, when he no longer got sullen to keep from crying in front of everybody, he thought about the driver. He hadn't even seen the driver, only the back of the gravel truck speeding on even faster down the road. The boy hated gravel trucks after that, the sight and sound of them. But he couldn't decide about the driver. Maybe he was somebody who would have been angry if he had stopped, maybe someone who would have kicked him for letting a dog loose on the road where gravel trucks belong. The boy couldn't hate drivers the way he could hate gravel trucks. But he thought about that driver, the tiny hollow eyes, the hair matted and long, the arms thin but the knuckles big and crusted from scratches and bruises, a red cold sore under his nose, a thick raspy cough.

# THE DREAM

One night the youngest boy dreamed that someone in his family would have to die. It was a law or something. He was not scared in the dream because there were many people in his family and he, the quiet one, seemed least likely. He figured he would be the last to go.

Then the whole family decided that he was the one who should die. He ran away through the cornfields with everybody chasing him. They had buckets of gasoline they were going to throw on him and burn him.

His oldest brother caught him in the cornfield and was laughing. The rest of the family came running up behind, with gasoline spilling all over.

Then he woke up.

The next day the boy took a closer look at everyone around him. They did not look like people who would kill him now. They did not even look quite like the family in the dream. It was just a dream, he thought. But he did not say, Pass the potatoes. He did not ask them for anything.

# THE ONE-ROOM
# SCHOOLHOUSE

The week before the auction the youngest boy walked to the one-room schoolhouse just before sunset when the barn swallows were swooping over the grass for gnats and the chickens were starting to roost and the cows were starting to chew their cuds—at that time of the evening when nobody paid any attention to where anybody else was. He kicked the schoolhouse coal door the way he'd seen the older boys do it and the way they must have seen other older boys before them do it. It was the secret coal-door kick and was as good as a key to the front door.

He knew this was his last chance to be in the schoolhouse before it was torn down or turned into a grain bin. It still smelled the same, which was bad, as if the last person to study here had opened the door to let in the smell of the neighborhood hog yards and then locked the smell in forever. Nothing looked any better, not the out-of-tune piano or any of the carved-up desktops. He opened the door to the library and found it about as small and interesting as the inside of a privy. He pulled out the bottom drawer of the teacher's desk and in it were the spelling, arithmetic, and history answer-keys for books that nobody wanted the answers to anymore.

No wonder nobody cared that next week some

strangers would come and buy the seats and the recitation bench, maybe even the piano and the library stand. The farmer whose property bordered the playground would get the land and the schoolhouse. Nobody would bid against him. They wouldn't dare. Let him have the land, make it part of his cornfield, which is what it should have been a long time ago.

The boy slipped out of the coal door and headed toward home. Grasshoppers too big for swallows fluttered up from the playground with their sounds that always reminded him of shaking a dry twig. He tripped on a pocket gopher mound and remembered that he never trapped pocket gophers on the playground because their mounds made such nice soft bases for softball. I wonder where the Gypsies will camp when they're heading up for the big harvests. I wonder where I'll go for my first picnic when I'm old enough for a girlfriend.

# PART III

ONE DEAD CHICKEN

# HABITS

They're something you do over and over again so you don't have to think about what you're doing every time before you do it. That's why you need good habits. So you do good things without having to think about them every time before you do them.

That made sense to the boys. But then one of them said, Like what, for instance?

Like putting dirty socks together and putting them in the hamper. Like brushing teeth before you go to bed. Like washing hands before you eat. Like combing your hair before you go out. Like tucking your shirt in. Like wiping your shoes at the door. Like closing the screen door so the flies don't get in. Like saying Please. Like feeding the chickens on time. Like closing cupboard doors. Or hanging up clothes, and not leaving your things in the living room, and cleaning your fingernails, and washing mud off your boots before putting them away, and not scratching mosquito bites, and cleaning the cat dish, and putting caps on straight, and wearing matching socks, and chewing food with your mouth closed, and wrapping food before putting it away, and making your bed, and passing food at the dinner table, and not slurping soup. Things like that.

And if it's a habit, you don't even think about those things anymore? the boy asked.

That's right.

I haven't thought about any of those things for a long long time, he said. I didn't know I had so many good habits.

# CHURCH BEARS

.

When the boys were very small, bears lived in the steeple of the church. If the boys couldn't sit still during the service, they would have to go up in the steeple. Maybe they'd sit still for the bears.

Every Sunday, just before services started, chimes played from that same steeple where the bears lived. This was supposed to calm the bears down, and if the boys knew what was good for them it would calm them down too.

It seemed that all the little kids in that church knew about the bears, so there must have been something to it. The boys never did see the bears, though they tried hard enough, looking up as they went into the church, thinking that one of the bears might show its head or paw over the bulwarks up there. They saw pigeons instead, ones that didn't seem too worried about bears. But maybe the bears were saving their strength for boys like themselves. Even if they never saw bears, sometimes they heard creaking sounds from the steeple that might have been a bear standing up or lying down. Doubting that there were bears didn't seem worth the risk.

Now and then the boys watched other little boys being carried out of church. Once one of them even screamed, Not the bears! Not the bears! but the boys saw him in one piece later after church. They didn't know for sure whether anyone had ever gone to the bears, never to be seen again. But who'd want to be first?

A few years later, about the time the boys discovered that storks didn't deliver the little pigs to the hog house, a nursery was put in the church basement. Now the families with little children didn't sit in the back pews anymore. They just turned their children loose in the nursery. No more talk of the bears. It was as if the bears were set free from the steeple the same week the kids were turned loose in the nursery. To the boys, it seemed that no little kid had really been to church unless he had been there when the bears were in the steeple. Sometimes the boys would sneak into the nursery after church and break a few of the little kids' toys. These new kids probably didn't have to worry about the steeple, but at least they would have to wonder what was big enough to rip the wheels off their racing cars and the heads off their teddy bears.

# ONE DEAD CHICKEN

In the neighborhood where the boys lived, people went to a very strict church. It was a church that taught that people are evil, and that if they were left to themselves the whole world would turn into a cesspool. If left to themselves, they would eat each other like dogs. Or worse. As the boys understood it, rules kept people from going all out in their naturally bad ways. Rules and punishment. Maybe the punishment even more than the rules.

But obeying rules was sort of like holding your breath. You could do it for a while if you really kept your mind on it, but sooner or later *poof!* and you'd be back to your bad old self. There didn't seem to be much middle ground. What you were doing was either good, like holding your breath, or bad, like letting it all out. A few games might be in the good category if they weren't being played on Sunday and so long as everybody was being a good sport. Which, they supposed, meant not feeling bad if you were losing and not feeling good if you were winning. Almost all work was probably all good because it almost always felt bad in the doing. What was hardest to understand was why things that felt so good while they were doing them could be so bad when looked at from the point of view of having been done.

I am so disappointed that you did that.

How could anybody be disappointed in a boy doing what made him feel good? He was just being his naturally bad self. Was he supposed to hold his breath and believe some kind of rule that was the opposite of what he really was?

One day the boy who was thinking too much about good and bad caught a chicken and stuck it head-first into a gallon syrup can full of water. When the chicken was dead, he didn't ask himself, Now, why did I do that? He asked himself, What can I do with this dead wet chicken? Which meant, Where should I hide it? He buried it in the grove and them came back out into the ordinary world where nothing looked particularly good or bad.

He was supposed to feel guilty for doing something terrible like that. He didn't. He was supposed to be punished for doing something so awful. He wasn't. When he looked around, he couldn't see that he was any better or worse than anything or anybody around him. Only one thing was different now, and that was this one dead chicken. And that didn't seem to make things better or worse. It pretty much left him back where he started.

# HOUSE VISITATION

Once a year the minister and an elder from the consistory visited every family in the church. The house visitation day was so important that the house had to be cleaned spotless and all the dandelions had to be dug out of the lawn. House visitation meant taking off overalls and putting on suits and ties right in the middle of the day in the middle of the week. House visitation was serious business, and the boys knew it.

Visitors and hired hands left when the minister and the elder drove on the yard. These men in black suits weren't coming to look at the crops or to talk seed corn, that was for sure. They were more like the IRS coming to check out the bottom line of everybody's hidden lives.

And how is your spiritual life? the minister was likely to ask after opening the meeting with a prayer that told more than it asked about how everyone was guilty even of sins they didn't know they had committed because they were born guilty. He would ask questions about family devotions, about taking the name of the Lord in vain, and about Sabbath Day observance. He would ask if there was anything that anybody knew in his heart that should be talked about. The elder would listen to the minister and then add a question of his own. Sometimes the elder asked the hardest question, like In what ways do you feel you have grown closer to God during the last year? The boys would sit nervously on the sofa, hoping the grown-ups would answer all the questions so that there wouldn't be any left for them.

But one year the youngest elder who had ever been selected in the church came with the minister. He believed in making people comfortable before the serious talk started. He chatted with the boys about baseball and 4-H. He asked them if there were any new pigs on the farm. He asked them about their new dog, Fritzy. He asked if Fritzy did any farm work.

Oh, yes! said one of the boys. He chases the pigs. He barks and chases them if one gets out!

Now all the boys were excited about telling the young elder about Fritzy's escapades. They interrupted each other in their excitement, each trying to add new dimensions to Fritzy's barnyard achievements. And in all this excitement, like passing gas in Sunday school by mistake, one boy blurted out, Yes! And Fritzy bit the boar in the nuts!

House visitation didn't turn out as bad as the boys thought it would that year. They never did stop blushing as they sat quietly on the couch, but the grown-ups answered all the minister's questions before he could even think of turning to the boys. The young elder sat quietly with his eyes wide and his lips tight. He looked as if he had been stunned by an electric cattle prod. Of everyone in the parlor, he looked like the one to whom God had spoken most directly that day.

# GYPSIES

·

The Gypsies were on the schoolyard again, same as last year. They had old army trucks, the backs covered with canvas, where most of the women and kids sat. You could never tell how many of them there were when they drove by in their slow caravan, always using a gravel road running parallel to a main highway, going north or going south, whichever way the harvest was.

Then at night, when they stopped someplace, all those trucks emptied themselves out with hosts of dancers and singers. Or at least that's how it sounded out there after the sun went down. So much happy noise with so little light to see what they were doing. Nobody knew for sure just what they were doing. Not noise so loud that anybody in the neighborhood could complain. Who'd dare to say, Stop that giggling, stop that chuckling, stop that sweet singing, stop that jingling? If any of the Gypsies ever got mad or mean, they were very quiet about it. Maybe they hid that part for when they were on the road. Maybe they fought in the backs of the trucks during the day. But not at night. All you'd hear were these happy sounds that made the farmers in the neighborhood uncomfortable, but what could you say? Sometimes one of them would even come out and ask if it was all right to use the schoolyard. What could a farmer say? He didn't own it. And even if he did, what kind of person could say no? And the Gypsies never left a mess. Next morning the schoolyard was just as if they'd never been there.

Sometimes one of the Gypsies would leave the schoolyard at night, always a young man, and all he ever wanted was to buy a few eggs or to trade one thing for another. Never very much of anything.

Then they'd be gone. One of the boys would try to hum one of the songs he thought he'd heard the night before, but could never get it quite right. Someone would say they saw dancing just before the sun was all the way down, but no one could ever describe the dance. How many were there when they all got out of the trucks? Numbers varied by the hundreds. Some farmer always said he was missing a chicken or a few eggs. But who really counts all his chickens and eggs? Nobody knew anything for sure. Did anybody even count the trucks?

# THE CONVERTS

A missionary came back from Nigeria with two young women who were believers now. The minister called them converts. They wore more clothes than they used to and they didn't have any use for drums anymore. They knew a little English now and had learned to sing two hymns. They stood up front in church one Sunday morning, both smiling as if they were happy about what had happened to them.

The boys had never seen anybody this black. They were black as bullheads. It was just the palms of their hands that looked lighter, and they were almost as light as the color of a bullhead's belly. Their faces and arms shone like they'd just come out of the water.

The minister introduced them. They were going to sing the two hymns they had learned—"What a Friend We Have in Jesus" and "Swing Low, Sweet Chariot." The organist played a little bit and they started singing. Their voices were like nothing that had ever been in that church. It sounded like a lion roaring in the hog house. They were terrific! They were so good they drowned out the pipe organ. They were so good people started swaying in the pews.

The boys started swaying too. One tapped his hand on the church bench, but some grown-up put a hand over his. Then the boys saw people elbowing other people here and there in the church, poking them to stop the swaying that was catching on all over the place. When the women stopped singing, the organ played on for a few minutes, louder than ever, as if it wanted to have the last say.

Then everything was quiet. Everyone was perfectly still and the women sat down. The boys felt like something terrible had just happened. They blushed the way they might if they had broken a window in the church basement or passed gas during congregational prayer. These women were dangerous, all right.

# TORNADO

It was just like they always said—a hot muggy day, the air too still at supper time, and then that big belly of a black cloud, a little band of sky beneath it, coming at them from the southwest. Everybody was phoning everybody, getting blankets ready for the cellar, then standing outside watching. When a piece of the cloud started to fall down across the sky below it like a section of hair working its way down somebody's forehead, the boys had to get into the cellar and stay there.

They sat in the dark in the middle of the canned tomatoes and applesauce, waiting for the grown-ups, who didn't come. And didn't come. They started talking about what they'd do if all the grown-ups got killed. What if only kids were in the cellars and all the stupid grown-ups from the whole neighborhood were getting beat together like a big cake or soup?

Then one of the boys got serious and said, Maybe we should pray.

What would we pray? said another—Now I lay me down to sleep?

But the cellar door opened before anyone could think of something to pray about.

You can come out now, said one of the grown-ups. It missed us.

So much for the tornado. Here it was, a Saturday night. The tornado had kept them from going into town and they hadn't even seen it. The tornado missed them to boot. And tomorrow was Sunday, which meant sitting in church half the day. They could just as well stay in the cellar.

But Sunday morning was livelier than they expected. The tornado hadn't missed everybody. It hit a whole neighborhood of Roman Catholics who lived to the west. It hit them good. And that gave everybody at the boys' church something to talk about before the service.

The boys didn't know much about Roman Catholics. They knew they worshipped idols. They knew they ate too much fish. They knew they drank too much and swore too much. They knew they gambled at bingo and went to worldly amusements like the movie theater and that they danced worldly dances. Dances other than square-skipping. They knew they played games on Sunday and sometimes did unnecessary work too. They had no clear sense of honoring the Sabbath. But what the boys heard people say before church that day made Roman Catholics sound so bad that it was no wonder the minister prayed for them.

The best part of that Sunday came after church when carloads of people wanted to drive to the Roman Catholic neighborhood and see just what the tornado had done to them.

It was worse than the boys guessed it would be.

This must be what Sodom and Gomorrah looked like after the Lord punished them, said one grown-up.

A manure spreader was twisted like a dishrag so that half of it was still right side up but the wheels were upside down, a roof of a hog house had landed about a half-mile from where it started, a piece of somebody's sewing machine had skidded across the road and stopped on the shoulder. There were lots of bedsprings and mattresses strewn through the fields and ditches, which made another grown-up say, What do you expect—what with all the kids they have?

The boys felt uneasy in the middle of so many Roman Catholics and their mess. There were lots of them out there, stacking up pieces of their buildings, rounding up the cattle that were still alive. Kids too, everybody pitching in as if they thought they could fix everything in no time flat.

Look at that, said one of the grown-ups. Even after such a terrible thing happened, they're still working on Sunday.

Which made the boys think a lot about sin that day, and what happens to you if you're on the wrong side and how when you're on the wrong side the good you try to do makes you even worse. The long and short of it was the boys didn't do any more chores on that Sunday than was absolutely necessary. They didn't want any Roman Catholic tornado coming down on their heads.

# HOOF ROT

Only his first year in 4-H and the boy had a steer that had a good chance at winning the grand champion ribbon. A perfectly marked Hereford, just the right amount of fat, just the right height.

The boy named his fine animal Duke and every afternoon taught him how to stand for the show ring. Then, two weeks before show time, Duke got hoof rot, big open cracks between the clefts of his hooves that looked like a bad case of athlete's foot. The veterinarian's ointments didn't help, only made Duke shiver and kick from the sting.

So the boy tried prayer. Dear Almighty God in heaven, he said. If You fix Duke's hoof rot, I will never say another swear word for the rest of my life. Not even a dirty word. For Jesus' sake, Amen.

Praying worked. The next day Duke looked normal. But the boy thought he may have prayed himself into a corner. God's side of the bargain came awfully easy and he wasn't sure his side would be like that. Maybe I should have said that I'd swear only once in a while, he thought, or maybe that I wouldn't swear in front of my grandfather.

Then the boy thought of another problem: exactly where do good words leave off and bad words start?

For God it was probably a matter of black and white—like hoof rot or no hoof rot—but a bunch of in-between words popped into the boy's head right away.

And what about saying nice words in a swearing way? he wondered. He knew some people who could do that. And he knew some people who could use swear words in a nice way. Maybe both ways were swearing. Maybe neither.

The boy tried to think of a loophole in his prayer. Did I say swear at or swear *period?* If I said swear *period,* then I could really be in trouble, because that might include swearing in my head without even saying a word.

The boy figured he'd better get the matter straightened out before the fair or God might come down on Duke right there in the show ring in front of the judge and everyone else. Break all his legs or something. In the meantime, he decided his best bet was saying as little as possible, avoiding talking situations, and really staying away from ones where he might get mad at somebody. To avoid too many questions, he said he had a sore throat, and was glad he hadn't promised not to lie.

He squeaked through the last week before the fair with hardly a mishap of the tongue, just a few gray words that weren't aimed at anyone in particular and probably wouldn't be considered swearing. At least not by everyone. Certainly not by the kind of people who would be at the fair, and the kind of people who hung out there should probably be the standard of right and wrong on this question.

Duke did not win the grand champion ribbon, but that hadn't been part of the bargain. He was reserve champion in his class—a kind of in-between winner. As the boy led Duke from the show ring, he saw that one of the healed hoof-rot cracks had opened just a bit. Not enough of a crack to affect the judging or anything. It was as if God had given him permission to loosen up a little, not to come out swearing with his tongue on fire but at least to enjoy the company of the fair people, and maybe trip over a few almost cuss words now and then without worrying too much about it.

# NIGHT HUNTING

The church where the boys went taught that it was bad to go to movies. The boys had talked to town kids from another church who did go, even to outdoor movies, where everybody could see who was attending. The town boys told them how much fun it was to sit in the backseat and watch through the windshield as the shooting started on the big screen.

The boys thought about this when they went night hunting with the men. The boys' job was supposed to be watching for the game warden—which meant watching for any car taking an interest in these headlights roaming around the fields or going too slow down the road.

There were two kinds of night hunting. One was where you ride down the road or through a level stubble field looking for jackrabbits. This kind sometimes meant trying to run the rabbits down with the car or at least driving at high speeds while one man leaned out of the window with his automatic .22 peppering away at the zigzagging rabbit and hoping to get a lucky shot. The other kind was slow night hunting, creeping along with the car through tall grass waiting for a pheasant to stick its ring-neck up for the one careful shot from a twelve-gauge.

One night they were going to be doing both kinds

of night hunting, first on the road, then through the stubble field to the slough grass, where the shooter would put away the .22 and load the shotgun.

The boys did glance around now and then for headlights, but they were more interested in what the men might be shooting. Most of the time they sat staring through the front windshield the way the town boys must have watched an outdoor movie, just waiting for the thrills to start. There weren't any jackrabbits that night, not even one, and the men started talking about whether there might be too many foxes around again. But then they made their way slowly into the slough grass. One man sat on the front fender with the shotgun and the driver drove slow. The boys never did see the pheasant head—it was too far down on the screen of the windshield—but the car stopped and the shooter aimed. There was the loud bang of the shotgun, the delicious smell of gunpowder, and then the driver turned off the headlights. This was procedure. Now the boys were especially supposed to look around for the game warden. The shooter got down off the hood and went feeling through the slough grass until he found the warm bloody feathers of the pheasant. He passed it back to the boys, then looked around over the horizon. There weren't any headlights, but one of the boys thought he heard a car engine in the distance.

This was enough to call off the hunt for the night. Slowly, they inched the car back toward the farmhouse with the lights off. The shooter held his rifle and shotgun outside next to the door, ready to toss them away from the car if the game warden's lights appeared. The boys sat in the backseat, ready to throw the pheasant away.

In this way, they made their way back to safety. It must have been like sneaking away from an outdoor movie theater without anyone from the church seeing them, one boy thought, but even with pheasant blood on his shirt and hands, he imagined how much fun the movie theater might be.

# THE NEW MINISTER

The new minister had just arrived from the Old Country. He had an accent but spoke good English and was a wonderful preacher. The congregation liked the way he rolled his *r*'s and the way he could make them feel bad and good in the same sermon, first by pointing out how great their sins and miseries were and then by showing the way to get rid of those sins and miseries. He was a big hit, but sometimes his words did not come out right during congregational prayer.

One Sunday he was praying for the church's missionaries in Nigeria. What he said in his loud, deep voice was, Lord, may it be Thy will to protect our missionaries in Nigger-ia.

Nobody in that church would ever laugh in the sanctuary. You don't laugh in church when the minister is preaching. And nobody did laugh at that.

But then there was the time that he was praying and meant to say, Lord, deliver us poor sinners from the fiery darts of the Evil One. But this time, what he said was, Lord, deliver us poor sinners from the diery farts of the Evil One.

Some people coughed in their handkerchiefs. Others made sounds that could have passed as little sobs.

Mothers pinched their children so hard that they looked more likely to cry than snicker.

The minister stopped just a second, as if maybe he was thinking about saying that another way, but then went on, But, oh Lord, not our will but Thine be done—which was his way of apologizing for the slip of his tongue.

After church, people agreed that the Evil One had gotten away with a lot in the sanctuary of the Lord that day. Even though the Evil One had really played some tricks on the minister's tongue, everyone in the congregation had managed to bite theirs, and not one real chuckle had been heard by anyone. And everyone had a good laugh about that.

# THE MINISTER'S WIFE

There were two reasons everyone noticed the minister's wife when she walked into church with her children—she had more children than anyone else and she was the most beautiful woman there.

During the worship service, the boys often stared at her and wished that she were one of those women who nursed their babies in church. But this beautiful woman was so shy it was not likely she would show herself like that in church. Or any place else the boys might see her.

One Communion Sunday the minister invited some of the congregation over to the parsonage for coffee after church. Services were always long on Communion Sundays, because it took the minister a long time to pour the wine from the big silver pitcher into all the Communion cups. The congregation drank the wine very quickly that Sunday, so the minister must have known they were ready to get off those hard church benches. He was being nice by inviting them over to the soft chairs in the parsonage for coffee. Of course, it would be the minister's beautiful wife who would have to make coffee for all those people.

The boys were standing in the porch watching all the grown-ups find chairs in the parlor when they saw the minister's wife go into the kitchen with her newest baby. Maybe she was going to nurse it! The boys peeked through the kitchen door. She was nursing all right, but she was so shy that even in her own kitchen she had covered her breast and the baby's face with a dish towel.

Later the boys came back for a second try. They smelled freshly brewed coffee as they sneaked up and didn't expect to see anything unusual. With one hand the minister's wife was lifting one cup after another, and with the other hand she was holding one of her breasts. She squeezed some of her milk into each of the cups.

Pretty soon she served the coffee to her guests. Everyone held the cups on their laps until all the guests were served. Then they raised their cups to their lips together, the same way they did in church with the wine cups, but now no one was saying it was in remembrance of anything. Everyone was nodding and saying nice things about the coffee. The minister's wife blushed, as she always did when the congregation showed that they appreciated her.

That night, back home as the boys were getting ready for bed, they started talking about the minister's wife and what they had seen. Then one boy said, Say, do you remember what it looked like?

None of them did.

I remember one thing, said the youngest boy. There were twenty-eight cups and nobody had to ask for more milk.

# GAS

Hold your nose! Here he comes!

In church, when he was preaching, there was a safe distance between him and the congregation. The window fans probably helped. Sometimes the big microphone at the podium picked up a few sounds that it shouldn't have, but the congregation had gotten used to this, and there was no way the radio audience could have known what it was.

But during the week when he was doing his pastorly work, he might pass gas at a bad time. Maybe when he was ministering to the sick. Or officiating at a wedding, right when the bride and groom were on their knees in front of him. Or even worse at weekday prayer meetings where people came to pray that the weather would get better.

One old man in the congregation thought this pastor was unfit for the ministry. What he does in people's presence is a sin! he said. By their fruits shall ye know them!

When the elders of the church told the pastor about the old man's complaint, the pastor's face got red and he said, May the fire of my soul be measure to the fire of my bowels! Bring this man before me. And for a minute the air in that small consistory room was clear and silent.

What do you know of spiritual matters? the minister asked the old man.

I know that it is not what proceedeth into a man but what proceedeth from him which defileth him, said the old man, holding his Bible in his hands.

The stench of your heart is filling this room, said the minister. Do not ye yet understand that whatsoever entereth in at the mouth goeth into the belly, and is cast into the draught? But those things which proceed out of the mouth come from the heart; and *they* defile the man. The minister opened the Bible to Matthew 15:16–17, which the old man clearly had not understood.

With that the pastor passed gas heartily. There, he said in the same kind of voice people use when they make their last payment to the banker.

At that moment the angry wrinkles left the old man's face, as if the winds had calmed over the raging sea of his mind, as if finally he knew he was in the presence of a holy man whose very life was a parable.

# YOU KNOW WHAT IS RIGHT

Before the boys went into town on Saturday nights, the grown-ups always warned them to stay out of trouble by saying, You know what is right. Always those words: You know what is right. After hearing the same warning over and over many times, the boys figured they really must know what is right. But when they were on the downtown streets, it wasn't always so easy.

One Saturday night the first thing that happened was some town boys gave them the finger and yelled, Hey, Stinkeroos, you got cow doo on your shoes!

The oldest boy answered quickly by giving them the finger too and yelling, Oh yeah, city fellow? Your underpants is yellow!

The youngest boy said, Yelling at them like that, was that right?

The other boys weren't sure. They walked away from the town boys thinking about it. Was that right? Was that right? they said over and over to themselves. A little later they stopped in front of a new-car show window. They leaned against the glass and looked up and down the streets, wondering what might happen next.

Stop leaning against that window! shouted the sales manager. The boys knew the man could tell by their work shoes and overalls that they were from the farm.

Inside, the man was showing new cars to a well-dressed couple who looked as if they must be town folks. Let's do a stinkeroo, said the oldest boy.

The boys made their plan. They got into the next car that the well-dressed couple would be looking at. The boys who could passed gas. Then they all slipped out and closed the car doors behind them. They watched from across the street as the couple got into the stinky car. The man looked at the woman and said something. Then the woman spoke to the man with an angry look on her face. They were blaming each other for the smell, all right. Then they got out and looked at the sales manager as if maybe he were the one who made the car stink. They shook their heads and left.

The boys tried not to laugh in front of the couple, but then the youngest boy said, But was that right?

This made one boy laugh aloud, and soon they were running down the street laughing. Stop! said one of the boys. I'm going to wet my pants!

But would that be right? asked another. Now they all laughed so hard that they were all afraid of wetting their pants.

The gas station john! one of them shouted. They ran toward it to relieve themselves. The oldest boy was the first one to the urinal.

Inside the urinal was a handful of change. It was the kind of urinal that has a few inches of water in the bottom, like a cup. Someone had dropped the change into the urinal and then urinated on it. If anyone flushed the urinal, the change would go too. But for anyone to get the change he would have to stick his hand into someone else's urine.

The boys looked at each other, and it was as if

for the first time that night a clear light went on in their minds.

The oldest boy reached into his pocket for some change, dropped it into the urinal, then stepped closer and urinated over the raised ante.

Me too, said the next boy, stepping up politely. And so, in turn, each gave his share of money and urine until the mound of coins glowed like a collection plate.

Now *that* was the right thing to do, said the last boy as he buttoned up.

# BUTTERFLIES

When the men were out working in the fields, it was easy to tell them apart. Even if you couldn't see their faces or if you weren't close enough to make out their size and shape, the way they moved was enough to show who they were. If one bent over to pull a thistle or leaned his elbow on a fence post, it was as if he were writing his name on the air in big letters—it was so clear who he was.

But on Sundays, when the men were dressed in dark suits and sitting on the church pews, they looked alike. All those suntanned faces up to the white forehead where the hat band started. And during congregational prayer when they bowed their heads together, they seemed to turn into plants that had budded in a field of straight rows. The only way you could tell who was who was by remembering where each one always sat.

But when the worshipping was over and they walked out of the rose-windowed church, they were like butterflies coming out of cocoons. All their different colors got brighter and clearer as they went back into the sun toward the sparkling fields. One by one in their own ways they became themselves again.

# PART IV

SCAR TISSUE

# THINKING ABOUT THE CITY

People who came from there were different. They couldn't sit still. First they would talk too fast. Then they'd eat too slow. They'd call dinner lunch, and they'd call supper dinner. They had to be told when it was time to go to bed at night and couldn't get up in the morning without an alarm clock. If they wanted to know something, they'd say Tell me instead of Show me. They'd smile when there was nothing to smile about. They'd help people who didn't need any help. They acted as if they thought everything they did would be taken the right way.

The boys watched these people from the city, and they didn't have to be told anything. They saw what they saw and they didn't like it.

But they didn't see the city, only the people who came from there. They didn't see what it was—what building, what noise, what stink in the air—that made people turn out like this. This jittery animal called a city person. These people who wore clothes that never seemed to go with what they were doing. Clothes that made as much sense as a bridle on a dog or a saddle on a chicken. These creatures who tried to be pushy and nice at the same time. Whose idea of a joke were they anyhow?

And how could they stand each other if cities were really as crowded as people said, with so many people on the street at one time that they were like a herd of cattle in a sales ring, with houses as close together as farrowing pens, and sometimes dozens of them living in the same building with only a little hallway between them? How could they stand being there, and how could they stand each other with their *nice nice* this and their *talk talk* that and their runny smiles all over the place?

# WHO DIDN'T WANT

# AN INDOOR TOILET

When times got good, everybody got indoor toilets. Most people kept the outdoor privy for when the weather was nice or for when their feet were too muddy to come in the house. But you had to be a pretty bad farmer not to be able to afford an indoor toilet too.

Except one rich farmer. He didn't want an indoor toilet.

When other farmers asked him why he didn't have one, he told them things like this:

Houses are places where you go to have good times with your family. To eat. To sleep. To play with your children. To make children. Now you people with your indoor toilets, what have you done to your houses? You put a place for people to shit in them and call it improvement! Think of this—somebody says, I have to go to the toilet, and instead of going outside they just go in the next room. Now how are the rest of you supposed to feel when you know that person is right on the other side of that door—only a few feet away—shitting! At least people with chamber pots could hide them behind the bed. But your indoor toilet is always there. Pretty soon your hallways smell. Then the porch. Even the kitchen! And you call that modern. You call that civilized. A house is almost a holy place. Now you tell me what kind of person would build a room for shitting in a place like that! Not even a dog shits in his own house.

Nobody could really argue with him. They just tried not to talk about toilets with him. Because when they did they couldn't help feeling a little bit foolish for what they had done to themselves and their houses.

# SCAR TISSUE

He stopped chewing on his cigar and laid it down next to the lantern. It simmered there on the burnt spot where he had laid other cigars. He picked out an egg from the bucket and rubbed at a spot with the damp dishcloth. He would start talking now. The boys sat at the edge of the hoop of lantern light and looked up at his face.

Well, I'm a pretty old farmer, he said. I can remember the days before rat poison. There was as many rats back then as good stories. Good talkers and good workers. In those days you could tell the speed of a man's hands by checking the scar tissue on his legs.

He held an egg up to the lantern light, as if he could tell this way which ones would be culled out at the hatchery.

One time we was shelling corn. Corn shelling. Five or six of us shoving corn in the hopper. We was going for a thousand bushels. Big crib. And big rats. I don't know how many. Lots of them. They was legion. We seen their tails slickering in the corn. They was digging right ahead of our scoops.

He laid an egg down and wiggled his short forefinger as if he could make it look like a rat's tail. He picked up his cigar, chewed on it, and laid it down on the burnt spot again.

First thing you gotta know about rats is they're
dumb, but they know when they're in trouble. The second
thing you gotta know is that when they're in trouble,
they don't run for light—they run for dark.

He adjusted the wick on the lantern. The egg
bucket was not quite half-empty. The boys leaned back
on their hands, still listening.

So we was almost to the bottom of this corn when
we run into them rats. First one trickles out. Then the
whole works. Like when one ear of corn falls out of the
pile and then it all comes down. So we start stomping. I
must of stomped a dozen of them when the fella next to
me misses one when he stomps. And that rat swickers
around real quick and comes at me from the side where
I can't see him. He's looking for a dark tunnel. And he
finds it. My pants leg! He sees that little tunnel over my
shoe and up he comes. I had on wool socks, the thick kind
that gives rat claws something good to dig into. Good
footing. So he gets his claws in my wool socks, looks up
the tunnel, and don't see daylight. He must of thought
he was home free for sure.

He paused and rubbed his chin while the boys
squirmed.

Well, you know, in those days, rats was always
running up somebody's leg. Specially during corn shelling. I guess it was just my turn. You just had to figure
on it a little bit during corn shelling. Like getting stung
when you're going after honey. You was always hearing
somebody yelling and seeing him kick his leg like crazy
in a corn crib or pulling his pants off so fast you'd think
he got the instant diarrhea.

Now let me show you the scar that critter give me.

He pulled up his overalls. His leg was white and

hairless. Just below the knee, on the inside calf, were a set of jagged scars.

That's how fast my hands was, he said. I grabbed that sucker before he could clear my shoestrings.

He rubbed the scars with the tip of his finger, gently, as if they were still tender.

There's the top teeth. And there's the bottom, he said. I grabbed and I squeezed. And I squeezed. And the rat bites. And he bites. I felt his ribcage crack, but his teeth stayed in me like they was hog rings. I guess we both got our way. Now he's still hanging there dead inside my pants while we killed the rest of them rats. Then I pried him loose with my pocketknife. Stubborn sucker. But he knew a dark tunnel when he seen one.

There were only two eggs left in the bucket. He rinsed the washcloth and took one more chew on his cigar. He picked up an egg and rolled it over in his hand, looking for spots.

Now almost any old farmer can tell you his rat story. They've all had a rat or two up their pants. But just ask him to show you his scar tissue. I can wager you this—the ones with slow hands won't show you where they got theirs.

# THE SEESAW

One man had this idea that he would build a seesaw so big that he would center it over the roof of his chicken coop. The crops had been bad that year and he said he figured, What the heck, I'm not going to be using half of my grain bins, I'll just tear one down and make a big seesaw out of it.

The other farmers laughed, thinking this was a pretty good joke. One said he wasn't going to tear his down, but fill it up with the government's unkept promises.

But when the joking stopped, the man started building his big seesaw. Down went one of his large grain bins and up went this strange contraption. If this man was joking, it was a joke he was ready to ride forty feet up. Half the neighborhood came to watch the test ride. The boys were there too, and one volunteered to be first, but the man said he'd test it himself. He loaded one side with sacks of feed. On the end that was sticking high up off the ground, he had a rope and pulley, and he had staked another pulley on the ground. He pulled the high end down and got on. Then he eased himself up, keeping the rope in his hand to make sure his seesaw didn't flick him into the air like a stone from a slingshot.

It worked. A seesaw that could give you a ride higher than a Ferris wheel.

Soon a man replaced the feed sacks and two men rode it together. Then two boys on one side and a man on the other. Then one boy on each side. Whenever someone was at the high point, people on the ground would hold the other side down so the suspended person could look around at the miles and miles of cornfields that had hardly earned their keep that year. By the end of the afternoon everyone there had ridden the seesaw. Then it started to creak and someone said they thought some nails were pulling out.

I didn't stop farming while I was ahead, said the man who had made the seesaw. But I think we should stop this while we are.

And so they did, taking it apart piece by piece and placing the lumber in the empty spot where the grain bin had been. Some farmers even offered to help rebuild the grain bin, just in case next year might come back with bumper crops.

For the boys, the seesaw was all the bumper crop they needed. Living on a farm wasn't everything, they knew that. And they knew they were missing more than a good crop—like a roller coaster in California that went out over the ocean, or skiing down mountains. The world was filled with great things they were missing—the Empire State Building, Old Faithful, the Eiffel Tower, what have you. But forty feet off the ground on a seesaw was, at least for the moment, enough of the world for them.

# POCKET GOPHER FEET

You could turn in a pocket gopher's front feet at the bank. There was a bounty of twenty cents a pair. The feet had to be dry or in salt so they wouldn't stink up the place.

Getting the bounty on pocket gopher feet was not easy money. The boys set a dozen traps every night. Digging down under the mound to find the crossroads. Then scraping out a little hollow to put the trap in and closing everything up airtight so the pocket gopher couldn't tell that somebody had booby-trapped its hallway.

The boys didn't mind so much if they caught a mean one. The kind that dug itself out, following the chain to the stake outside, and sat there waiting for them, hissing, one foot in the trap, but ready to take on the world with its long front teeth. Mean ones were the easy kind, and the boys could put them out of their misery with one whack of a baseball bat.

The bad kind were the ones that were afraid to die. One of these might pack the dirt around the trap so tight that the boys couldn't pull the trap out. Or it might set its three free legs into the dirt so deep that the boys would yank the trapped foot right off. Or one of this kind might beat the boys to the punch by chewing its foot off and leaving it there in the trap before the boys got there.

So what do you do with one pocket gopher foot?

Just because a pocket gopher wanted to live so bad that it pulled or chewed one of its feet off didn't stop the boys from trying to get their money. The first time they found themselves one foot short of a pair, they brought the single foot in for the bounty, thinking that the woman in the bank wouldn't notice. But she did. Where's the other foot? she said.

We only caught one foot, said the youngest boy.

Sorry, the woman said. The bounty is for both feet.

Couldn't we get half a bounty for this foot? asked another one of the boys.

The woman would hear nothing of it. So the boys saved the foot and the next time a gopher left one foot in a trap, they put it in a sack with the first one and brought the two feet in for the bounty. They figured the woman in the bank wouldn't notice that they were not a perfect match. But she did. These feet don't match, she said.

My socks don't match either, said the youngest boy, but these are both my feet.

Look, said the woman, moving the mismatched pocket gopher feet around with the tip of her pencil. They're both right front feet. No bounty for these. And I will thank you if you don't try to fool me again.

The boys saw that the county knew what it was doing when they hired the woman in the bank to take care of pocket gopher bounties. They went home with their mismatched pocket gopher feet. They didn't throw them away. They knew there was a slim chance they might catch the other foot of those pocket gophers some day. The odds weren't very good, but they seemed better than trying to fool the bank woman.

# PIES

It was always good to visit that lady because she made such good pies. What was so good about them was the little waves on the edge of the crusts. The boys could tell how big a piece they were getting by counting those little waves. Eight waves was a big piece.

How does she do it? the other ladies asked. No one knew.

The boys walked over to her house early one day before everyone else went over there for fresh pie. They stood outside her kitchen window and watched her making her pies.

When the lady had the crust rolled out in the pie pan, she reached into her mouth and pulled out her false teeth. Then she took them and pushed them down on the pie crust all the way around. So that's how she made all those nice little waves that everybody liked so much!

Pretty soon everyone came for fresh pie.

What beautiful pies! all the other ladies said.

The boys did get eight-wave pieces that day.

Every now and then, between bites of that good pie, the boys looked at the lady. She was watching everyone eat and grinning a big grin.

# SHEDS

Down the road lived a man who was an odd one. He built seventy sheds on his farm. Little sheds, where he could put little things everyone figured could go somewhere else. Whenever he had something he wanted to put away, instead of looking for a place for it in one of his buildings, he built a special little shed to put it in. When he bought a new lawn mower, he built a new shed for it. When his dog had eight puppies, he built eight little doghouses for the new animals. He had a little shed where he put tin cans. He had one for old shoes. This man had built a separate shed for chicken feathers.

But one shed, way back in the grove, painted bright red with white trim, was his secret shed.

What does he keep in that red shed in the grove? everyone wondered.

The boys sneaked out there to find out, but the red shed had a big lock on it. And no windows to see through.

So they went to the man and asked him, What do you have in your red shed in the grove? He was a friendly enough man, so they thought it would be all right to ask.

But the man got angry when the boys asked him this and said, That is none of your business, none at all.

When the boys went back to check the shed again, the man had put another lock on the door and a sign that said KEEP OUT.

Let's climb up in one of those trees and wait, said one of the boys. Maybe he'll come by and unlock the door.

They climbed the tree and sat on branches where they could see the man's shed.

Pretty soon he came out there. He was carrying two keys. He knelt down in front of his shed and unlocked one lock. Then the other. He opened the door of his secret shed.

Inside was another shed! A blue one that had a lock on its door, too. Then he opened the door of the blue shed, and inside was a smaller yellow shed! And inside that a green one! The man was down on his knees opening door after door of his little sheds. Pretty soon the boys couldn't see where his hand was going. And all those little sheds, one after another, looked like a rainbow, and the boys couldn't see where it ended.

# YELLOW GIRL

When drainage tile was put in the bottomlands, corn
could be planted where only slough grass grew before.
But the tile drained the pond too. The boys couldn't remember when ducks and bullheads swam there, but the
pond was still surrounded by willow trees and made a
good place to get away from everything. They'd go down
to the pond and look for old bottles and badger holes, or
they'd make dust castles out of the pond bed.

Then one year there was a big flood and the pond
came back in spite of the drainage tile. When the waters
went down, the boys walked to the pond to see what it
looked like with water in it. They brought fishing poles,
figuring that wherever there was water there would also
be fish. Cornstalks and trash from all over the county
hung in the willow trees, and the pond was brimming
with muddy water. They fished for an hour and now and
then saw ripples in the water that told them something
alive was in there. But they couldn't tell what.

Then one of the boys hooked something. It didn't
fight much, but it was big enough to bend his pole like a
horseshoe. The boy managed to pull it slowly toward the
shore. They were expecting a big mud turtle, and they
had their sticks ready. Then part of the catch showed

itself on the surface, a large rolling motion, like a big fish turning over on its back as it swam.

I saw its yellow belly! shouted one of the boys. It's a giant catfish!

But it wasn't a catfish. It wasn't anything alive at all. It was a dirty dress the flood had brought from somewhere. The boys took it off the hook and laid it out on the shore. It was a girl's dress. When they squeezed the water out, they could see that it was yellow, with small red flowers. It had two pockets, and white buttons at the neck. The boys fastened the buttons and checked the pockets. They were empty.

The dress lay on the shore and the breeze started to dry it. The colors became clearer and brighter as it dried and the hem ruffled a little in the breeze.

As a joke one of the boys drew a head over the dress. The other boys joined in, scratching legs and arms in the soft dirt. There, one of them said. There's our yellow girl.

The boys left her lying there, knowing there was little chance that such a flood as the last one would come and wash her away. They went down to the pond often that summer, always saying they were going fishing. And they did catch a few small bullheads. The yellow girl stayed in place through the summer, and when the weather changed her at all the boys fixed her up again by retracing her head, arms, and legs in the dirt. They came to think of her as their Sleeping Beauty, though nobody ever stooped to kiss her.

# THE GOOD HIDER

This woman liked to hide from her husband. It's not that she didn't like him, and she didn't have to be in an angry or sad mood when she hid. She just needed to be in a hiding mood. It could happen anytime. Maybe the husband would come home from the fields and she wouldn't be in the house. Or he might turn over in his sleep to be awakened by the cold place on the sheet where she should have been. Then he would go down to his easy chair to see if she had hung her apron on it. This was her way of telling him that everything was all right but that she'd gone off to hide.

Right away the husband would start his hunt. She would leave him a few clues. Maybe a kerchief on a fence she had climbed. Or a barn door left open just a bit, like a little grin. But after that she was a good hider. She was good at making herself look like the place she was hiding. On sunny days when her long hair was blond in the sunlight, she might hide near the straw stack where her hair would look the same color as the straw. On a rainy day she might hide in a willow tree where her long wet hair would hang down to look like wet willow branches. Or she would stand in the shape of a small apple tree in the orchard with an apple in each of her outstretched hands. Other times she would hide among

146

animals, making herself look and sound like them. Once she hid in a pen of sleeping sows, lying down among them with her hands and feet in front of her like the legs of a sow. And she made the snoring noises of the sows so well that the animals didn't notice that she was there among them.

But the husband was as good a seeker as the wife was a hider. He knew how to look and listen for what was *not* there: like the branch that should have been moving in the wind, or swallows that should have been singing, or crickets chirping. He'd walk on the paths that seemed least walked on and stop and listen at those places that seemed the least noisy. When he thought he was getting warm, he stood still and held his breath. If she was holding her breath, he'd hold his longer. If she was making sounds of the animals nearby, he'd hear the little giggle that wasn't an animal sound.

When she was found out, she would leap up or down like a flushed partridge or pouncing cat from her hiding place. She came at him wild and laughing. Even when he was expecting it, she scared him, and he would turn away running as fast as he could. She always caught him in a few steps. As he knew she would. Just as she knew he would find her.

# THE BIDDER

He was the cleverest bidder at the sale barn. For years only the auctioneer and the man in the ring knew how he did it.

When the kind of cattle that the bidder was likely to buy came into the ring, half the men in the sale barn might watch him, all of them trying to figure out how he signalled his bids. Does he bid by touching his cap? By lifting his thumb—the only finger on that hand he hadn't lost in the corn picker? Or does he just frown a certain way? It was no use. No one could tell how he bid, and so no one could have the fun of bidding him up on something he really wanted.

Most big bidders were fat, but he was a skinny, jittery fellow who was usually very busy fidgeting his hands, shuffling his feet, twitching his lips, or shifting his eyes. Some people thought that was his secret—that he was hiding his bid somewhere in all his jitteriness. In fact, when he did make his bid, it seemed harder than ever to see that he had done anything unusual.

It was one of the boys who finally said, He doesn't do anything when he bids. At first the men ignored the boy's remark, but then they noticed it too—the only time the bidder was not doing something was when he made a bid. After a while, as word got around, everyone could tell what the auctioneer and the man in the ring could tell all those years—and that was that when the bidder wanted a cow or calf or ringful of steers bad enough, all the busyness of his body stopped and he sat still with simmering desire. That was his way of bidding.

The boys didn't know what other people learned from that. But they knew what they had learned. The world was full of bidders, they figured. If they watched close enough, they'd be able to see it. Even when people pretended they didn't want something, they were probably bidding for one thing or another almost all the time. Figuring this out probably wouldn't make life all that much easier, but they'd watch for it.

# WHO KEPT ONE

# HAND IN HER POCKET

There was a woman who always kept one hand in her pocket. When she was in the garden weeding, one hand was hidden in her pocket. When she was feeding oats to the chickens, she scattered the grain with one hand and kept the other in her pocket. In church. In the store. Wherever she was, one hand was always in her pocket.

The boys wanted to know why this was so. They asked people, but no one else knew either. So they came up with a plan, a trick to make her show that hand. They would lay a string where she walked and trip her with it as she passed by. When she was falling, she would have to pull her hidden hand from her pocket to keep from hitting her face on the ground. Then the boys would run out to help her get up—but really to get a look at that hand.

They started talking about what they would see. It had to be more than just a withered hand. She had to be hiding something better than that. Maybe she was clutching a big black pearl, one of them guessed, or a rose carved out of a ruby. Something so pretty that they'd never guess what it was.

The boys laid out the string one day, but when

the woman walked by, they couldn't make themselves pull
it. If they saw what the woman was hiding, she might
give it to them. And if it was as beautiful as they figured,
they might have to walk around the rest of their lives too
with one hand in their pockets, hiding what she'd given
them.

# WHO GREW SNAKES

## IN HER ORCHARD

One old woman grew snakes in her orchard, then paid the boys to kill them. The boys got good at this job, catching the snakes with sticks that had forked nails on the end. They slipped these down over the snake heads and picked them up unhurt.

The old woman wanted to see the snakes alive before she'd talk money. So the boys brought them to her in gunnysacks, and she'd look in to see the squirming garters blaming each other for their misery. She'd sputter and puff when she saw them, but she'd bring her money. Ten cents apiece.

The boys pulled out one snake at a time so she could count them. Then they hit the snake heads with rocks, right there on her sidewalk where she would see it all. When they finished, the old woman paid them, and they put the bloody snakes back in the sacks.

Once they were out of view of the old woman's house, the boys emptied the sacks on the ground. Most snakes still squirmed a little, but after doing this a few times the boys could tell which ones would make it past sundown. The live ones they took home and kept in the cellar. The next morning one boy worked table scraps into the mouths of the survivors with the eraser end of a pencil. If a snake swallowed, the boys carried it out to the pasture where it wouldn't be able to find its way back to the old woman's orchard. It wouldn't be fair to the snake or to the old woman if they killed the same one twice.

# WHO LOOKED UNDER HIS CAR

He drove an old black car that he always kept spotless and polished. He drove it slowly and it looked like a big black insect as it moved dark and shiny down the road.

Before he got into it, he always stooped down on his knees and looked under it. First he knelt behind the car and looked toward the front. Then he knelt in front of the car and looked toward the back. He did this slowly, the same way he drove. When he got to where he was going, he looked under it again from both ends.

The man was very rich and did not have a wife. He had very large ears which lay flat against his head and were hairy inside. The boys laughed about his ears. Everybody did.

Once the boys crawled up behind the car when the man was in the store. They looked under it from both ends but didn't see anything different. When they stood up, though, and saw themselves in the shiny surface, they couldn't help looking at their own ears. Then they ran away from the car, and when they stopped they checked each other's ears.

They watched the man come out of the store,

watched him look under his car from both ends and drive slowly away.

Look at those ears! said one of the boys. Just look at those ears!

# THE OLD WAITRESS

A very old waitress with a long gray braid worked in the cafe. The boys listened to the men joke about the gray braid, teasing her that its color never changed and that it never got any longer or shorter. Everybody knew it was a fake. You could even see where the bobby pins held it to the back of her head. But the braid wasn't the only thing about this waitress that didn't change. When people walked in, she always greeted them with the same word. She always said, Order?

There were many ways men would answer that question: Order be a law against this weather! Order in the court! Order day I drunk too much!

When she wouldn't respond, one would say, Hey, she's out of order!

The old waitress acted as if she didn't notice the men's jokes. She wouldn't even look at them until they ordered food. Some of the men seemed to think she liked their *order* jokes, but the boys knew she was at least as ornery as she looked with her fake braid cutting the air behind her like a cattle whip.

The boys didn't go to the restaurant to eat. They came to watch while the men laughed, and didn't really notice anything but the old waitress's fake braid. They didn't see how wet her whistling was when her face was close to their coffee, didn't notice that she sometimes carried their silverware in her armpit, didn't even see her little smile when she held the metal milk-shake container under the mixer a lot longer than it would take to mix ice cream and milk. A lot longer.

# THE OLD MAN

Why didn't anyone pity the old man, even when he was crossing the street? With his slow, shuffling limp, he'd back up cars and trucks for a block. Why didn't they at least give him a cane and say, Here, try this—it might help you?

Every Saturday when the boy came to town, he'd see the old man, same overalls, same bedroom slippers, same gray hat. He was fat, not just his stomach but his rear too, and he had a big fat nose and those little crusts of spit or whatever in the corners of his mouth. And he'd blow his nose by turning his head and putting a knuckle against one nostril to shut it off while he blew out of the other one.

The boy always stared at the old man who, when he wasn't crossing the street in front of traffic, sat on the bench in front of the implement store. But the boy stared as much at the people who should have been staring at the old man. Why didn't anyone pity him? Why didn't they do something about him? Or did they think he'd die soon?

The boy figured the old man would die soon. But he didn't. He was like one of those broken limbs you think is going to break off the tree but just goes on hanging there with most of its leaves dead—but not all of them.

Once the boy sat down next to him on the bench. The old man smelled like the inside of an old cigar box, the kind that nobody ever throws away, that gets used for pencils for a while, and then for nails, and finally disappears—but then shows up again when you don't expect it, maybe with some candy in it.

The boy looked at the old man again. Other people were walking by as if there was nothing to look out for, as if everything was the way it ought to be. The old man just sat there, smelling like a cigar box, ignoring them too.

# NEITHER COMING

## NOR GOING

There was the man who didn't shave like the other farmers around there. He didn't grow a real beard, but he never had a clean shave either. Just this straw-colored stubble that made him look like a rough character.

The boys had been a little bit scared of him when he drove up in his green pickup to talk to the men about the crops or to borrow something. They figured this bristly fellow was up to something. Something about him was out of kilter, that was for sure—what with that weird beard. Then one day he drove up faster than ever and jumped out of his pickup as if something important had just happened.

Betcha don't know what happened at my place, the boys heard him say. When he had the men's attention, he put one foot up on the hog yard fence and lit a match on the bronze button of his overall suspenders. Cigarette smoke circled around his hat and through his whiskers while the men waited to hear what happened.

Sow with thirteen pigs and only nine tits, he said. He sniffed and then spit ten feet out into the hog yard. Know what I did? he said. He rubbed his stubble with the hand that still had a cigarette between the fingers.

The men waited to hear what he did.

I let 'em fight it out. He pinched his nose with

the cigarette hand, squinting to keep smoke from the tip of the cigarette from getting in his eyes.

You'd think the littlest ones would lose, wouldn't you? he said.

You'd think so, said one of the men.

Nope, he said. The little ones hung in there. Even one runt. Fought like there was no tomorrow. Thought them pigs were going to tear that sow apart. Sometimes there'd be two, three going for one tit. Hammering away at her like woodpeckers on a fence post. Never saw the like. There was sow milk and pig spit and straw and what-have-you just a-flying around there. Bloody ears and a couple of nipped tails. I tell you it was something. They knew what they wanted and didn't care if there wasn't enough to go around. Those little suckers would pee on the run just to beat the next guy to an empty tit.

So how did it end? asked one of the men.

I didn't stick around to find out, he said. That's not why I'm in farming.

He stamped out his cigarette as if he were in a hurry again. He pulled a wadded handkerchief from his pocket, blew his nose, and drove off.

Wonder why he did go into farming, said one of the men.

He's not so scary, said one of the boys.

# WHO DIDN'T LIKE

# MEAN TOMCATS

This man didn't like mean tomcats. Once he saw two of them fighting and got so angry that he cinched each of their tails to a different end of a rope and threw the rope over the clothesline.

The tomcats went wild, clawing and biting at each other where they hung upside down facing each other in midair.

The man did this to the tomcats in front of some neighbors. The men looked surprised at first, then tried to make this terrible fight seem like something they'd seen before. One said, Better than a cockfight, and another one said, More like a raccoon and a badger.

The boys were also there. This was worse than anything they'd ever seen, and different too. They looked at the cats. They looked at the men. They looked back at the cat fight until they couldn't anymore.

Stupid, one of them said.

Gross, said another.

They walked away. Then a few of the quieter men walked away too, before one cat was dead and the other one was as good as.

The man who didn't like mean tomcats must have noticed that the boys and some of the men didn't like what he was doing. The next time he saw a mean tomcat he held it with rubber gloves and stuffed it headfirst into a dusty boot. This way there wasn't so much fur flying and the mean tomcat died with hardly any fuss. The man had waited until he had an audience, but this time all the men stayed, a few even thanking him for getting rid of the nuisance. The boys stuck around too. What they saw wasn't totally new to them. Like drowning a gopher, one of them said.

# PART V

GOTCHA

# GOTCHA

The boys had seen him only once, but they remembered him years later. If they ever met evil, he was it. Those gap teeth and dirty thick hands. That snotty laugh and that white dome of a bald head. He was big and slimy and sharp all at the same time. He should have been in a fairy tale and eaten by a good dragon, one bite at a time. Or he should have been tied down and covered with honey for the ants to eat. He should have choked on raw eggs. Buzzard eggs.

But he had been dead for maybe two, three years now and no one talked much about him. He didn't seem to mean much to anyone else, one way or the other, but he was the man who had caught the boys stealing watermelons from his neighbor lady's garden. Caught them and made them stand in front of the lady saying they were so-o-o sorry and would never do it again. Those weren't even his watermelons! And the boys had only taken two little ones that weren't even ripe! The lady would never have missed them. That man had ruined their Saturday night—and every other Saturday night they went to town for at least a year.

Good people don't catch boys stealing watermelons from an old lady on a Saturday night. They just don't. Good people have better things to do. Good people don't crawl on their hands and knees through the tomatoes to catch boys stealing two measly little watermelons that weren't even ripe and that were small enough to hide under a loose shirt. Good people don't jump up from behind the tomatoes with hairy arms and a head glowing like the moon and a dirty slobbery laugh saying, Gotcha gotcha. Good people don't take boys by the collars and shove them to the front door of an old lady's house on a Saturday night, ordering them to say, I'm so-o-o sorry, I'll never do it again.

Good people let boys steal two lousy little watermelons from an old lady on a Saturday night. Good people just let them do it! Then maybe years later they tease the boys about it. Maybe at their wedding, or at a picnic where people are eating watermelon and having a good time. Everybody would laugh, and by that time the boys who'd done it would have their own watermelons and they'd give some to everybody. That's what good people do.

But no, not Mr. Gotcha Gotcha. Getting killed falling off a ladder putting up the neighbor lady's storm windows was too easy for him. At least he could have fallen on a spike and suffered a little. Maybe got gangrene or something. Gotcha gotcha. I'm so-o-o sorry. You bet.

# DEHORNING

Nothing could be worse than dehorning cattle. Not just the blood that covered their faces and ran down over their eyes and nostrils. Not just the sound of the saw cutting through the base of the horn. Not just the metal dehorning chute clamping against the sides of the animal and holding its head between the two bars. And not just the bellowing and snorting when it tried to pull free. But all of these together.

Sometimes the boys tried to act brave by standing around waiting to pick up the horns when they fell to the ground. Or they held the ointments and salves that were supposed to stop the bleeding when the job was done. But sooner or later the dehorning got to be too much for them and they found an excuse to walk away.

If they went off to the grove to play on their model farm, they took turns pretending they were a steer being dehorned. One got down on his knees. Another held wedges of wood scrap on his head. Another used a wood file as a saw. Together the boys screamed and bellowed the sounds of dehorning while they pretended to file the wood scraps from each other's skulls.

Doing this, the boys learned what cattle went through. They learned that the animal could see the horns sticking out from its head, those strange pieces of itself that moved whichever way its head turned. The boys learned what it felt like to see one horn fall to the ground and then see the dehorner move with his saw to the other side for the one that was left. Sometimes they poured water over the head of the one being dehorned so that he could learn what it felt like to have blood running down his forehead and into his eyes and nostrils.

# WHAT ARE THEY MISSING?

There was a kind of boar that went on breeding even after it was castrated. It had a hidden testicle that you couldn't see from the outside, so there was no way of telling which boar was hiding this little secret.

But it was no secret when that animal set itself to work on young gilts that were meant for market instead of breeding.

Look! That one has a hidden testicle! one of the men would shout, and everyone would jump helter-skelter into the pigpen with sticks and feed scoops, smacking and pushing the busy boar off the female before the damage was done.

The men separated this kind of boar from the other pigs, but the boys noticed how the men, instead of punishing that animal, gave it more and better feed than the others. Once the boys watched a man stand next to the animal's special pen for nearly an hour, talking quietly to it and stooping over now and then to stroke its ears.

For the boys, the mystery was not so much in the strange boar as in the men. After all, where their own testicles were located was pretty ordinary. What do the men think they are missing? the boys wondered.

# THE SILAGE PIT

The boys went with the grown-ups to the house the day before the funeral. It was their cousin, and he was only four years old. Yesterday he had drowned in the silage pit that had filled up with water after all the silage had been fed to the cattle. You could see the silage pit as you drove on the yard. It just sat there now, with no excitement around it, just a lot of green water between two low cement walls. It didn't look like a swimming pool. You'd have to be four to even think of wading in that water.

The boys thought everyone would go straight into the house where people were crying together about the little drowned boy. But no, only the women went to the house. The men walked out to the silage pit first, and the boys went with them.

You wouldn't think it was that deep, one of the men said.

Another pointed. They say he might have been trying to float out there on that post.

You'd think he would have yelled when he was in trouble.

They say nobody heard a thing. His dad finally walked in when they couldn't find him. He stepped on the body, but it was too late.

The men went on and on like this, trying to figure out exactly what happened, then walked to the house to join the little boy's family.

The boys stayed near the silage pit. They saw the father's footprints in the mud along the edge. Over the fence they saw the cattle that had gotten fat on the silage that wasn't in the pit anymore. The water was green like silage. The water smelled green. It looked like a place that frogs or snakes would crawl into. How could cattle eat anything that had come out of a silage pit? What could a little boy have been looking for in a place like this?

# THE COYOTES

# ARE COMING BACK

There weren't supposed to be any coyotes out there any-more. The last ones had been killed with cyanide traps years ago. Coyotes? Not out here. We know how to take care of coyotes. The ones that walk on two legs and the ones that walk on four.

But there was howling in the night. Just a little bit. As if a coyote had wandered out there to test the air. Did you hear a coyote last night? A few people did. The rest laughed. Then some people started making coyote sounds at night to make fun of the ones who heard the real coyote sounds. Soon the idea that there was a coyote out there was just a joke.

Except to the boys. They went out to find the coy-ote. Not only did they find pheasant feathers that a coyote had left, they found coyote hair on the barbed-wire fence! A few gray hairs. The boys knew they were not from any animal they usually saw around there. So where was that coyote now?

The boys walked the line fences where the grass was knee-high. Not there. They walked along the railroad track where there were small willows and rosebushes to hide under. Not there. They walked along the creek bed. Not there. They looked down the corn rows and in the alfalfa fields. Not there. They climbed the windmill, where they could see for miles in all directions. Not there anywhere. In all their looking, the boys hadn't even seen a coyote track. All they had were some pheasant feathers and a few gray hairs. They knew these wouldn't prove anything. They threw the feathers away but kept the coyote hairs in a small jar where they could look at them whenever they wanted to. They took turns sliding the coyote hairs between their fingers and trying to guess what a whole coyote would look like.

The boys figured the coyote was being shy and hiding so well because it didn't trust anybody in its new neighborhood. They decided to change that. They brought a dead chicken to the spot where they'd found the pheasant feathers. The next morning there was nothing but chicken feathers. They brought out a dish of milk and a dead rat. The next morning these were gone. Then they brought a pork chop and some strawberries. And as they were leaving, they saw the coyote. Standing in the alfalfa field watching them. It didn't run. It just stood there as if it knew they were the ones who were bringing food every day.

Wow! Look at him! Look at those ears! Look at those legs!

The boys had never seen a wild animal that big in the fields out there before and stood watching it while it watched them.

Now what do we do? said one of the boys.

We'd better tell the grown-ups to set cyanide traps, said the oldest boy.

# THE GOOD-LUCK NECKLACE

When the old bitch had another litter of pups, because none of them looked alike, the men guessed there were as many fathers as there were offspring.

She must of run with a pack of wild dogs when she was in heat. You'd never guess these critters were brothers and sisters.

The boys listened to the men talk about bad breeding and were afraid the men were going to kill the pups. And the boys had to admit that the litter looked pretty bad. Some were spotted and some were solid. One had big paws and the others small. Some had brown eyes and the others blue. Some had short noses and some had long. But the biggest difference was in the tails. When the pups were nursing, the boys saw the wagging tails were all different colors and shapes.

Let's cut the tails off, said the oldest boy. That will make them look alike.

The others agreed this was a good idea, so they took the pups one at a time to the chopping block. The oldest boy had the ax, but he was so afraid of cutting into the pups' hindquarters that he swung wide and chopped off only the tips of their tails. When he was finished, the blunt tail ends made the pups look even worse.

When the men saw how foolish the pups looked, they pitied the boys for trying so hard to save them and promised not to kill any.

This did not make the pups look any better, but it did make the boys proud of what they had done. So proud that they found all the tail tips and strung them on a cord as a good-luck necklace.

# THE WELL

The boys were told to stay away from the well, not to
play on the planks that covered it, not to lift the planks,
not even to think of looking down in the well or throwing
things into it to see how deep it was.

Then a young steer climbed up on the planks and
fell tail-first right through them. The boys heard the old
wet lumber break and the loud, hollow sound it made in
the mouth of the well, almost like a big version of somebody popping his finger out of his mouth. Hearing that,
they looked up to see the big-eyed look on the white face
of the steer, its hooves clinging to the edge of the well as
if they wished they were fingers, and then a mooing
grunt, hoof-scraping sounds on the inside of the well, and
a flat-sounding sort of *sploosh*.

The boys were disappointed to find that the well
wasn't all that deep. They could practically touch the
steer's nose, and if one of them had fallen in, they could
easily have gotten him out. It was hard to pity a steer
who had just stumbled into something they weren't even
allowed to touch.

But now they had the chance to prove that they
could be trusted around the well. Trusted and then some.
They knew they'd have to tell the men before they got
the steer out or no one would ever believe their story.

But they wanted to have things in hand before they yelled for help.

The stupid steer at least knew which way was up, its nose pointing straight at the boys. Wedged in with all four of its legs pointing up and its head between them, it looked stupider than ever. But it was easy to drop a lasso around its neck, then another and another and another. Now the boys wrapped the ropes around their backs, stood in a circle around the well, leaned back and pulled.

It wasn't going to be easy. Because the well got tinier and tinier as it went down, the steer's rear quarters and back were stuck as tight as a cork in a bottle. But they had a good start in their rescue mission, that was for sure. They had the right idea, nobody would be able to deny that. So they called the men.

The men were impressed, once they saw that the boys were telling the truth about a steer in the well, of all things. They just added a little finesse to the operation, roping the steer's legs so that when they pulled up, the legs would take part of the weight and wouldn't catch on the side of the well. Then they brought a tractor with a manure loader on it, tied the ropes to the loader, hoisted the steer up and lowered it back to the ground. Ten minutes was all she wrote.

The steer looked no better for the wear, big patches of hair scraped off its flanks, but the men examined it by waving their arms to see if it would stand up. It almost fell over at first, then walked away, sniffing the ground as if it were embarrassed.

That was a close one, said one of the men.

Sure was, said the oldest boy. Good thing we're not so stupid as to play around that old well.

# THE GIRLS

The girls were having all the fun. They'd made a tent by hanging a blanket over the clothesline. They had dolls. They had little mud pies with ground corn sprinkled on top for frosting. They had dress-up clothes and old hats, even hat pins. They had high heels.

There were lots of people everywhere—cousins and uncles and aunts—and lots of food on the picnic tables. A softball game was going on, and after that there'd be a tug-of-war. But out on their end of the lawn, away from the grown-up games and food, the girls were having all the fun. Their pretend house, their mud pies and dress-up clothes were the best thing going, and the boys knew it.

Let's ask the girls if we can play with them, said one boy. But the others said, What—and dress up in high heels?

Instead, one of the boys ran by and jerked the blanket so that one end of the girls' house came off the ground. And there they were where everybody could see them, sitting in a circle with their dolls and mud pies and dress-up clothes, laughing and having a wonderful time.

Stop it! one of the girls yelled, and then a grown-up came by and told the boys to go play ball and get ready for the tug-of-war.

They did, sulking away to where they were told to go, rubbing the softball in dog droppings and spitting on the tug-of-war rope where the next person would have to hold it.

# NATURE'S WAY

When it was time to butcher roosters, the men told the boys to catch the roosters and said the oldest one could chop the heads off. The oldest boy was happy to have the most important job and ran to get the ax. But when he came back, he couldn't find the chopping block.

Everyone started looking, and then someone remembered they'd burned the chopping block in the old cook stove last winter when the oil furnace went off.

I can't chop the roosters' heads off without a chopping block, the oldest boy said to the men. You'd better make me another one.

Let's see now, said one of the men. That old cherry stump got rotted out, didn't it? Those willows aren't big enough, and we sold that oak log two years ago, didn't we? Course we cleared out that stand of ash to make room for more corn.

Everyone looked around. There were no logs left on the farm. And no trees that were big enough to make a chopping block.

You'll just have to figure out a new way of doing it, said one of the men, and they left to do the field work.

The oldest boy ran to the house and returned with a butcher knife. One of you hold the wings and feet, he said. I'll grab the head and cut it off with the butcher knife.

The youngest boy held the rooster, but just when the oldest had cut through the neck, the wings and legs beat so hard that the headless rooster got loose and jumped wildly in the air, spraying blood over everyone and getting bloody mud all over itself when it hit the ground.

This isn't going to work, said the oldest boy. The cutting part is easy, but a rooster's too hard to hang on to when its head's cut off.

So he figured out a way to give each boy the right job to match his strength. He held the rooster, most of the other boys did the catching, and the youngest boy cut off the heads.

Later the men came around to see how the boys were doing. The youngest boy had gotten very quick and sure of himself with the knife, and his arms were covered with blood. There were baskets filled with dead roosters ready to be carried away to be skinned.

Isn't it something, said one of the men, the way nature takes care of itself if you just leave it alone.

# DEAD POSSUM

One cow looked just like it was smoking a cigar. A piece of cornstalk sticking out of its mouth, steam like puffs of smoke coming out of both nostrils.

Look! said one of the boys. That cow's smoking a cigar!

The other boys thought it was pretty obvious. The cow did look as if it were puffing away, almost as out of habit.

So what? said the oldest boy. Tell us when the barn lays an egg. He was remembering the time eggs dropped out the side of the barn, about ten feet above the ground. Some chicken had selected an odd place for its nests next to a knothole.

There wasn't much that could happen that day that wouldn't have made one of the boys say, So what else is new? The weather was cold, the chores were taking too long, and there wasn't any snow to play in, but the frozen ruts did make walking enough work for two. The air was a cold kind of wet that makes your legs get chapped above your boots. So cold you needed gloves if you weren't working, but not cold enough for gloves if you were. At best, it was the kind of weather to catch a cold in.

The boys didn't have to tell each other that they

were in a bad mood. But then the weirdest thing happened. The boy whose job was to check the level of the big cattle drinking tank found a dead possum floating in it. This might not have been so interesting, but the dead possum had a big red apple wedged in its wide-open mouth. It looked like somebody with a big mouth who had been bobbing for apples. Somebody with a big mouth and sharp little yellow teeth.

The boy wanted to yell for the others to come see, but knew they wouldn't believe him or, even if they did, wouldn't be in the mood. One of them would probably say something like, A dead possum with an apple in its mouth? Why don't you ask him to share?

This was one weird thing the boy would have to savor by himself. He stood wondering about the possum for a minute. It must have stolen the apple from the orchard, got it stuck in its mouth, then come to the tank to get a drink or to try washing the stuck apple out. Maybe with its mouth wedged open like that it couldn't keep its nose above the water to breathe.

The boy lifted the dead possum with a hayfork. It was heavier than he expected, probably from drinking so much water. Two cows walked up to see what was happening. Then several more, until the boy was surrounded by cows. He flipped the dead possum out of the tank. It landed hard on the frozen dirt, but the apple stayed wedged in place. He poked at the apple with the fork, but it wouldn't come loose.

Isn't this something? he said to the cows. Isn't this something?

Some nodded, then stepped past him to drink.

# DEMOLITION DERBY

The dilapidated cars crawled around the baseball diamond like old curs or runt pigs that hadn't been fed for a week. They sputtered little clouds of blue exhaust, and their growls choked into whimpers. Then the loudspeakers blared "The Star-Spangled Banner," the crowd yelled and whistled, and somehow the beastly old cars revved to life. The drivers aimed at each other. They all looked happy but mean. They were going to make these jalopies sing their swan songs, and they liked it.

The clattering and crunching started right off. Bumpers came loose. Tires blew out. Radiators spewed steam. A few cars quit before anyone even rammed them, almost as if, in the middle of the bedlam, they'd died of fright.

The boys had never been to a Demolition Derby before. They knew the one rule—the last car that can still move wins—but it didn't look as if any of these old cars could either give or take much more damage than they'd already got. Some drivers chased other cars in reverse, trying this way to bash in radiators while only denting their trunks. A couple tried staying out of the fracas at first, sneaking around the edge of the field while the eager ones beat each other up, but sooner or later everyone's turn came. Only one could survive, and the boys knew it.

Who do you cheer for? they wondered. Should you cheer for the big bully Buick with fenders like over-stuffed shoulder pads, or for the skidding little Ford that tried to blind the others with the dust it kicked up?

The longer it went on, the derby got uglier, and it got harder and harder to want anyone to win. Some cars looked as crippled as three-legged dogs. One had its fender rubbing against a tire and sounded like it was screaming in pain every time it moved.

Who could be proud of winning this game? What would they have to show for it? The boys had that strange feeling of being bored and scared at the same time. Whose idea was this anyhow?

# THE RAT CAGE TRAP

There was a wire cage trap for catching rats. It was a kinder way of catching rats than the regular trap that clamped down on one of their legs and tortured them until a cat found them trapped like that or a person came by and beat them to death.

But once the boys took a cage trap with a rat in it and set it on a fire they'd built from corncobs. When the rat saw the fire, it must have known something terrible was going to happen and ran around the cage squeaking like a rubber-mouse toy. When the boys put the cage on the fire, it tried to climb the side of the cage and for a moment even hung upside down on top. But the flames still got to it and made its hair curl like tiny springs. It lost all its sense and ran right into the hottest part of the fire, where it clung to the cage while the fire did its work. Then it stiffened, as if it had gotten a shock, and the boys shoved the cage off the fire before the smell was too strong for them.

Only after the thing was done did the boys get uncomfortable. It wasn't as if anybody liked rats. Everybody hated them. Nothing was too bad for a rat. Name one good thing about them. But nothing the boys could tell themselves helped. They tipped the rat out on the ground and one of them took it on a spade and hurried to bury it in the grove. Others ran for water to put out the fire. Then they took the cage down to the stock tank and washed off all the charcoal and rat skin, looking around all the while to see if anyone was watching. They knew they must have done something awful, but they couldn't quite put their finger on what it was.

# JUNE BUGS

They'd hit the kitchen window at night like little stones.
Or more like cherries. But June bug heads were harder
than cherry skins and their wings were like tin. They
didn't splatter. Really, there was no sound quite like the
sound of a June bug hitting a window. Just as there was
no sound quite like the sound of milk hitting the bottom
of an empty milk bucket.

But when one of those little pellets, or whatever
they were, hit the kitchen window for the first time in a
year or so, more often in May than June, one of the boys
always said, Where did we put them?—meaning the Ping-
Pong paddles.

Old Ping-Pong paddles were best for swatting
June bugs as they dive-bombed the light of a kitchen
window, the kind of Ping-Pong paddle where rubber has
worn down to bare wood. This gave a good smacking
sound even louder than a June bug hitting the window.

To the boys, June bugs were kamikaze pilots and
the lit window a battleship. If a bug got past, the ship
sank. With their backs to the lit windows, the boys stood
like gunners watching for the little glitter of June bug
coming out of nowhere in a dark, split second.

The grown-ups watched this sport from inside,
laughing, saying that Ping-Ponging June bugs was good

practice. Someday that good reaction time will keep a hand out of the power take-off or the corn-picker rollers. An eye that can pick a June bug out of the dark will have no trouble spotting pinkeye in the feedlot or a weasel in the chicken coop.

The boys didn't think any farm work required quick anything. But June bugs were another matter. They put you in a swing-or-die world in a hurry.

# WHAT IF

What would happen if you lit a fire in the haymow, took one of these matches and lit the hay here by the door, then sat in the door and yelled Fire! Or you could yell Help! and see who came running.

But what if you couldn't get the fire put out?

You could put it out. You just stamp on it with your foot and it goes right out.

Nothing came of the talk that morning. It was just an idea. But a week later the boys found some twelve-gauge shotgun shells in the toolshed. If you give it a shake, one of them said, you can hear the BBs inside.

So they decided to get the BBs out. They peeled open the end, and out came the little black BBs. Then they noticed the shell was still not empty.

How do you get the rest of that stuff out? one of them asked. He stuck a nail inside the shell and got the little paper wadding out, but the dark, packed gunpowder was still inside the shell. They put the shell in the vise, then hammered with a nail, trying to chip the gunpowder out. It wouldn't chip out, but at least it didn't explode. They didn't know the little cap on the other side where the firing pin hits is what makes the shell explode.

Something distracted them, maybe a rat, or hunger, or boredom. They left the shotgun shell locked in the vise, where the men found it later, along with the hammer and nail. They figured out what the boys had been up to right away. They released the shell slowly, trying not to squeeze the firing cap. Their hands shook. They knew what might have happened, and they relived for an instant their own boyhoods—remembering the tree that fell the wrong way, the rope they almost didn't get loose from a friend's neck, the ice that was just as thin as they were told it was. All those moments of curiosity or ignorance that might have killed them. They chatted with each other about their own adventures, dropped in a few nervous chuckles, then coached each other toward anger and the work to be done.

# TURPENTINE

# AND CORNCOBS

It wasn't the boys' idea. They liked the stray dog, even if it did stink and look mean. Maybe it was growling because its paw was swollen—and maybe the paw had buckshot in it from the last farmer who saw it. The boys watched the dog standing by the water supply tank with its nose like a witching stick pointing at the water pipe.

The boys had heard the men talk about a killer. About dead sheep and young calves, their little throats torn and little tongues eaten. They heard talk about wolf or coyote blood in mad dogs. The boys had also heard the click of the gun chamber closing, and seen the open box of shells close to the porch door.

The poor mutt the boys saw didn't look like a tongue eater. Before the guns could get to it, the boys went out to water and feed that dog and put Raleigh's Black Horse Salve on its swollen foot. That's how they found out for sure the dog wasn't a killer, but there was no way they could hide the dog's looks with a little food and water and salve on the swollen paw. They remembered another idea they learned from the men, and coaxed the dog into the toolshed where no one would hear its whimpering and snarling when they held it down and rubbed its rear end with corncobs until it bled, and then splashed turpentine on the tender spot.

That's how they made sure the dog got away, howling and running to who knows where. Maybe all that pain would lead it straight back to a home it had somewhere, or at least to the river bottom with all its bushes to hide behind and all the little field mice just sitting around waiting for something to happen.

# THE HARVEST

At harvest time, things didn't go on in their usual way. The women came out of the houses and gardens wearing gloves, overalls, and shoes that were too big for them. But they were ready for work, ready to bring in what everyone had been waiting for.

Where did they learn to do all of these things? You never saw them on the tractors at other times. And now here they were, even driving catty-corner across the picked cornrows at just the right angle so they wouldn't bounce off the seat—where'd they learn that trick? And for the oats harvest, somehow they knew how to shock bundles in perfect little teepees all over the stubble. They didn't try setting up four bundles at a time, but the bundles got set up—and set up so they didn't tip over in a wind. Some of them even pitched bundles, maybe not as fast as the men, but they were fussier about getting the oats' heads pointed into the threshing machine in a straight line. And who taught them to keep the cattle from sneaking out when they drove a load of grain through an open gate? As strange as they looked in those big clothes, they didn't waste any steps.

The men joked about how funny the women looked getting on a tractor or bending over in the field, and the boys laughed along with them.

But at night, when the women had to quit early to cook supper and clean up the houses, the boys moved in to take their places, figuring that at harvest time the fields would be as friendly to one hand as another. They couldn't throw bundles with the kind of muscle the men had, but they got some work done by trying to remember the way the women did it.

# PLAYING SOLDIER

The boys decided to play soldier and to use feather darts for weapons. The long tail feathers of pheasants sank into the soft part of a corncob as easily as a quill into an inkwell—and that was all there was to it. A corncob pheasant-feather dart that took to the air like a store-bought arrow—and these didn't even need a bow, just a good throwing arm. The boys counted out their ammunition so that both sides would have the same number, spread out behind outbuildings and machinery, and started throwing feather darts at each other.

Maybe the beauty of the sleek brown feathers arcing through the air kept the boys happy for a while, but no one was getting hit and they didn't have any rules that would say what would happen if somebody did get hit. For all their ammunition, this wasn't much of a war.

So they agreed that a hit on an arm or leg was a *wound*. A hit on the rest of the body was a *dead*. A boy with a wound could keep fighting but had to crawl to do it. A dead boy had to lie down until the game was over.

The two sides moved closer so there'd be a better chance of hitting somebody, but the cheating and arguing started as soon as the first dart grazed its target. My shoulder's part of my arm, so that's a wound! the boy shouted.

Disagreements over the rules became so great that the boys started hurling their darts harder and harder, standing closer and closer as they threw.

I suppose you're going to tell me that's your butt, said one boy as he nailed an opponent on the cheek.

Corncob darts had a little more bite to them than the boys expected. Scrapes and bruises started to flare on arms and faces.

The rules were rewritten in anger: Anybody who says Ouch is wounded, the biggest boy announced. And anyone who cries is *dead!*

It wasn't long before they all either hurt so much or were so angry that they added spitting and kicking to their arsenals. They tore the feathers out of each other's ammunition and stomped on each other's cobs. They wrecked their weapons and got a good start on each other.

A few days later it was as if the war game had never happened. They were back to the safety of their toy tractors and wagons, sometimes even helping each other fix whatever was broken. The scrapes on their faces could easily have come from rolling in the hay. The squirrels could have left those broken corncobs behind after robbing the corn crib. And maybe a fox had been killing pheasants again. Look at those feathers, all crumpled up like that. It's a wonder you didn't see any blood.

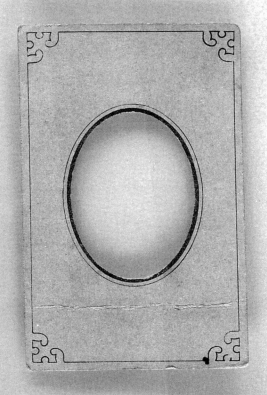

# PART VI

THE GRANDFATHER

# FIREFLIES

The boys realized later that only their grandfather knew
how dark the night was going to get when he invited them
for a walk down to the slough. I think I will have a surprise when we get there, he said. That was enough to keep
them from teasing him or each other while they walked.

The sun was setting behind them, making the pasture and cornfields a deeper green than ever. When they
came to the lowland where the slough grass followed the
bend of the creek through the fields, they felt the first
little patches of cool air flutter out of the grass and touch
their faces. Then came even cooler wisps of air as small
baskets of mist formed around them. You'd feel it on
your forehead first, just below the hairline, and then the
ears.

Their grandfather walked and talked in his quiet
way that kept them from complaining about wet shoes,
or gnats, or the cooling air.

Now, wait, he said at the edge of the slough.

Already the world was darkening around them.
The sky looked light, but when you looked down at the
grass, you could tell that down there darkness had already happened. Their grandfather drew an empty fruit
jar from the bag he carried.

I'm going to show you a little trick, he said. This fruit jar will be our flashlight on the walk back.

It would be easy for their grandfather to make them look foolish if they asked a foolish question, so they waited, watching quietly for the secret behind the trick. Whatever it might be.

The first hint was a sudden green glow in the dark grass, then a brighter, clearer light as the firefly rose.

Wait, he said again. Just wait. And as they did, the lights of the slough came on, one after another, until the air was swimming with tiny lights. Fireflies everywhere, rising from the moist grass like bubbles in a bowl of darkness, swirling as they rose, sometimes like bubbles going out in mid-flight and rising again from a new place.

Now, he said, just tease them into the jar, gently, like this. And they did, touching the bits of light into the fruit jar, dozens and dozens of fireflies, until there were inches of them. Their grandfather put the lid on loosely and held the jar toward one boy's face, which lit up with the glow of firefly light.

He held the jar toward the ground, as if this were the only way he would know where to step, and started back, holding the light next to his leg for the boys to follow.

To the boys, it felt as if they were on a secret mission, and they didn't talk until they were nearing the lights of the farmhouse.

Wait till they see this, said one of the boys. Just wait till they see this!

But the grandfather stopped. We're going to have

too much light once we get back, he said. And who knows who might be getting lost out here.

He took off the lid.

But no one will believe us if we don't show them the firefly flashlight, said one of the boys.

That's part of the fun, said the grandfather, and set them all free.

# THE FOREST

When the grandfather returned from his trip out West to see relatives, he had big news for the boys. He took them on their usual walk down the path between the cornfields and the pasture. He reached for a corn tassel, rolled the pollen in his hands, and sprinkled it across other cornstalks as they walked. Then he said, Would you believe there are probably more trees in the world than stalks of corn?

The boys looked at the half-mile-long rows of corn, all the tassels swaying in the sun. Hundreds and thousands of corn tassels as far as their eyes could see.

Their grandfather told of travelling through mountains where all he could see were miles of slopes longer than corn rows covered with trees. Trees, trees, trees, he said.

Where did they plant the corn with all those trees? asked one boy.

There was no corn in the forests, he said. Just trees, trees, and more trees.

Didn't that get boring? asked the boy.

Their grandfather reached for another corn tassel, held this one to his nose, then rubbed it between his palms more slowly than before. Yes, he said. That's why I came back early.

# THE OCEAN

Their grandfather told them that after he crossed the ocean and took a train to the farmlands, the grass on the plains reminded him of the ocean. But the grass on the plains was gone now and the boys didn't understand.

Does the cornfield look like the ocean?

No, no, he said, and laughed. The ocean doesn't come in rows, it comes in waves, and the smells that come with the wind off the ocean are nothing like the smells that come with the wind over the cornfields.

Is it really as big as they say?

It's bigger, he said. Look at the sky, and then think of something much bigger than that.

But in pictures you can always see a boat, or rocks, or an island. In pictures the ocean looks smaller than a cornfield, where you can't see the other side.

The ocean is wider than all the cornfields put together. It is deeper than a cornfield is long. And it has power, said the grandfather. Riding those waves you can just feel how much power is under you, around you, behind you. The ocean made me feel very small. But the corn—well, look, I'm almost as tall, and I could walk all the way to the end and back in half an hour.

The boys stared out across the cornfield. Then they looked at their grandfather. Could those old feet have stood above such great depths? Could those eyes have crossed more distance than all the cornfields in the world?

If the ocean's so big, could it ever come here and get us, cover all the cornfields and everything?

I don't think so, said the grandfather. The ocean *is* big, but I'm counting on the cornfields.

# THE MOUNTAINS

The boys had never seen a mountain. They listened to other people talk about them, how they rose up on the landscape fifty miles before you got to them, how the sun fell like a carpet of flames behind their spires. They told how the mountains would raise their arms through the clouds and how lazy clouds would tear themselves in two passing too low over the peaks. There were avalanches that came down like a hay bale on an ant, and cliffs so high that if you fell off one you'd have time to read the whole Bible before turning into a grease spot on the rocks below. Mountains were as strange to the boys as dragons, as fierce and as far away, as impossible and alluring as anything they had ever wanted to see or touch.

Mountains were not something they talked to each other about. They would listen to mountain talk together, but they thought about them in silence, usually alone and at sunset, when the same sun that set on mountains sank slowly on the long horizon of alfalfa and oats and corn, when barns and silos ten miles away would look like little cut-outs on the horizon, like little ants on molehills trying to make themselves look like something. Or when a storm was approaching, they'd imagine

that the thunderheads were like mountains, and they se-
cretly wished that each storm would bring an avalanche
of hailstones that would change everything in their puny
world.

# SNOW

There was so much snow. Would it never end? Snow down the chimney, snow on the windowsills. Snow high as the fences the calves now walked over aimlessly. A little mountain of snow inside the porch by the crack in the door. Snow on the roofs. Dirty snow. Clean snow. Snow on top of snow. Wet snow on the sunny south sides of buildings. Drifting snow on the north. Slopes, ravines, plateaus of snow.

Someone said it was pretty.

Someone said it brought out the best in people.

Someone said it would give people time to do what they should've done a long time ago.

Someone said it was good for next year's tulips.

What if you were me? thought the youngest boy. What if you were me and you had to go out there right now and milk a cow? What would somebody who isn't me think it would be like to be me right now? Putting on these leaky five-buckle boots, putting on this coat with last night's milk and manure caked on the sleeves, blowing into these old gloves to make a couple of finger holes warm? And have to walk through all that snow, plowing and shoving through all that snow just to milk a cow? I wonder what that person thinks I feel like right now.

# SKIING

Catalogs showed the boys what was happening in the rest
of the world. Snow skiing was one thing. People on big
hills with long skis and wide smiles, having fun.

Barrel staves were the only thing the boys could
find on the farm that looked like skis. They already had
snow, plenty of it, but what to do about the skis? They
went back to the catalog, then back to the barrel staves.
A strap of leather in the middle made a place for a boot,
and this made the barrel staves more like catalog skis. One
boy tried them on. He looked like a tall rocking chair, but
it was a start. Now all they were missing was a hill. The
biggest one they could find was a huge snowbank, but
this made for an awfully short ride. So they tried towing
each other around with a long rope, the pullers running
as fast as they could, then pulling toward one side so that
the skier swung out. It was like playing crack-the-whip,
and the skier got a pretty good ride. But the pullers got
tired too soon.

It's hard to have as much pull as a good hill, they
decided, but there was the tractor. They tried the same
crack-the-whip idea with the tractor, pulling the skier in
a circle until he started swinging out, then locking one
back wheel of the tractor so that it went in a tiny circle

on one spot and the skier whirled around like a stone in the kind of sling David used to kill Goliath.

Out on the end of a fifty-foot rope—who knew how fast the skiing boy was going? It was faster than anything he had ever felt, too fast to see or even imagine what was coming, too fast to keep his eyes open, too fast to hold on very long before the knotting muscles in his fingers and arms grew numb and let go and he went barrel-staving across the field like a hurled stone, sometimes skipping across drifts like a stone on water.

No smiling skier on any mountain could have had a ride like this! The boys knew that. They knew there was probably no skiing in the world could match what they did on barrel staves. But they also knew they needed that catalog. Just show us. Just show us someplace, anywhere, and we'll be there.

# DON'T YOU EVER FORGET IT

So what would happen if you didn't milk a cow some miserable cold morning and just turned her out with the ones that had been so well milked that their udders hung down like empty mittens?

*Dairy cows are meant to be milked on schedule, and don't you ever forget it.* That's what they always said.

But what if we did forget it? Just what would happen? And who set the schedule for five-thirty morning and evening anyhow? You can bet that was no cow's schedule.

The cows were always sleeping in their stanchions when the boys stumbled in on those cold winter mornings when the sun wasn't even up yet and their own nostrils had frost in them by the time they got to the cow barn. Stumbled in and took a few minutes to warm their hands between the cow's flank and udder before she even woke up. Not even cold hands would wake her. No way was this a cow's schedule.

So just what would happen if we skipped a few, just didn't milk them, maybe dump a bucket of water in the milk tank so nobody would notice there was less milk? What would the cow care? She'd probably go on sleeping instead of standing up to have some cold, milking-machine teat cup suck the warmth out of her. That milk was probably keeping the rest of her body heated so she could sleep better.

What would happen, really, if we just forgot a few and turned them out? Would the milk drip away like four leaky faucets? Would the cows roll over on their backs in the snow and spray like sprinklers? Or would their teats turn into Popsicles?

*Dairy cows are meant to be milked on schedule, and don't you ever forget it.*

You bet. Whose schedule is this anyhow? One of these days we're just going to skip a few and see what happens. One of these days we'll just see what difference it makes.

# POPCORN

It didn't feel like a night for being a hero. The boys had pulled the doors of the hog house closed tight against the blizzard, so inside, in that cold still air, you couldn't tell how bad it was until you moved your fingers in your mitten or breathed too fast. And it was getting worse— you could feel it inching in from the walls. How were the boys supposed to keep a whole litter of newborn pigs alive in this kind of weather?

They stood behind the sow where she lay, far enough back so she couldn't see them watching. Their job was to stay until she was through farrowing, to make sure every newborn pig found a pap to nurse and everything was all right before they came to the house.

The sow had built a pretty good nest, straw stacked up over a foot high around her—as if she knew how cold it was going to get. But it was colder in there than the grown-ups would have guessed, and the boys knew the baby pigs needed more help than a straw nest could give in this terrible cold. They did what they could, slipping their mittens off every time a new pig was born. At least those baby pigs would get some warmth from their hands before the cold air got to them. But this was bad, afterbirth freezing in the straw, pigs shivering, fighting to get close to what little warmth the sow had left. At this rate, their tails were going to freeze off. They were turning into little shriveling clumps against the fat belly of the sow, their wrinkled little bodies looking like kernels on a big ear of corn.

They're all going to die, said one of the boys, and it will be our fault.

They didn't want to ask for help. They weren't about to go running to the house crying, saying the baby pigs were going to freeze and they didn't know what to do. Instead they got a big metal grain basket with the rope handles, packed the bottom with straw, grabbed all the newborn pigs before the sow knew what was happening, and ran through the blizzard to the house with their basketful of pigs. They set it on the stove and turned up the heat. The pigs lay shivering in the bottom of the basket. Maybe they were too late. Maybe the cold had already frozen all the life out of them.

But the grown-ups said this was a good idea and told the boys not to worry. They could go to bed now. But they were barely in bed when they heard these clickety-clack sounds coming from the kitchen.

Popcorn! shouted one of the boys, and they rushed downstairs. But it was only the newborn pigs' little feet hitting the sides of the metal basket. They were heating up all right, and fast.

That's not fair! shouted one of the boys. We thought you were making popcorn.

Now the grown-ups felt sorry for the boys, so they set the lively little pigs safely on the floor and cooked up a batch of popcorn big enough for everybody.

# THE TONGUE INCIDENT

It was one of those things all the boys knew about—you don't put your tongue on anything metal when it's freezing outside. It will tear the skin right off your tongue, everyone knows that. And if you don't want the skin torn off your tongue, you just stand there with your head locked to the metal, looking like a woodpecker with its beak stuck in a tar roof. Or worse. And who'd want to help somebody with his tongue stuck to a metal doorknob, say, or a milk can? No matter how much it hurt, everybody would laugh, the way they would if you stuck your finger in a mousetrap or peed on an electric fence.

Everybody knew how stupid it would be to put your tongue on freezing metal. So the boy waited until he was alone to try it. He knew that most of these stories were never as bad as people said they were. They were stories people made up just to keep kids scared. He waited until he was alone and then leaned slowly toward the metal latch on the hog house door. He would touch it with the very tip of his tongue, check it out, the way he might check out the bathwater with the tip of his toe. He barely touched the latch, leaving a little dot of ice on the metal. His tongue was fine, just as he suspected it would be. Now he collected some saliva in his mouth and lapped at the latch in a big tongue-sweep, the way a dog goes for an ice cream cone.

The metal caught his tongue in what he thought would be a big safe lick. It was so quick. Quick as a mousetrap, quick as a bee sting, the latch had him in a tongue lock. He leaned back slowly, expecting it to snap off with a thin layer of ice for him to melt in his mouth. But it didn't. Leaning back felt the way his scalp might feel if someone slowly pulled his hair. And if he jerked back, he figured not just the skin but his whole tongue would go.

Keeping his tongue still didn't hurt much, but it was really cold. So cold it felt hot. He tried saying a few words to himself just to see if he could do it, in case he'd have to call for help—even though anybody who came would stand there laughing until he ripped half his tongue off. The best he could get out, though, was a long, airy Ahhh. He managed another sound that seemed to come through his nose, but this sounded so much like a pig squealing that it wouldn't get anyone's attention. Everybody expected pig sounds to come from the hog house.

What happened was that the boy started to relax. No matter what happened, this was worth it. To be here by himself, locked to the hog house by his tongue, was something that only he could have done. It was his trick and only his. Only he knew what really happened when you put your tongue to freezing metal. Everybody else was just guessing. Instead of pulling, he leaned into the metal latch, put even more of his tongue onto it and his lips too, letting them attach themselves. He blew, sucked, slobbered, and, in this way, let himself go.

He stood back and saw he had left only frozen spit on the door latch. He put his fingers to his face, touched his cold tongue, still happy with what he had done—neither wishing that he was, nor regretting that he wasn't, standing before an audience of laughter.

# PROGRESS

Everything was getting modern, what with a big freezer
in the porch that could hold half a cow and two pigs, a
bushel of sweet corn and enough rhubarb to keep your
mouth puckered until spring. Lights in the middle of the
night, sometimes where you'd least expect them and
wouldn't even want them. Behind the barn, for instance.
But the boys had gotten used to these. They'd been a few
years in coming.

Don't tell us about progress, they said to their
grandfather. We've been there too.

You have no idea, he said. You boys have no idea.
I saw a man go crazy because the mosquitoes were so
thick. They looked like a cloud, and he was in the middle
of it. He went plumb crazy. And I've seen women come
out of their sod houses in the spring to change the stuff-
ing of their corn-husk mattresses, and the mice would
pour out like potatoes from a bucket. You think you've
seen progress? I'll tell you, in those days we wanted progress and we wanted it bad. Progress was D-Con and DDT.
Progress was what killed things that used to make life
miserable. That's what progress was.

The boys thought about that. Weed spray for
thistles they once had to dig out with little spades. Head-
lice shampoos instead of hours spent under somebody's

nit-picking hands. Poison corn for gophers they once drowned out of their holes for a measly ten cents per bloated corpse.

The boys saw what he meant. But they were all feeling a little bit miserable, out on the edge of the grove where he was showing them what kind of mushrooms to look for.

Something is going too fast nowadays, their grandfather said. I'm not sure there was enough misery in that slough to plow it up.

The slough had been gone for only a few months and, sure enough, it seemed almost everything had changed.

What about the frogs and fireflies they used to catch—before the drainage tile was put in this year and the slough turned belly-up and the creek straightened out like a zipper across the fields and all those little critters were gone in two months flat? What about the crawdads and garter snakes and the big beetles and the swamp ghosts and all those dragonflies they used to catch and the hundreds of June bugs that hit their windows in May and the badgers that dug holes in the side of the old creek and that owl they saw in the willow tree in the slough and the muskrats they threw stones at? That wasn't even a year ago. Progress had come so fast they'd hardly had the chance to see how all those creatures could make them miserable. Progress might at least have left a few cracks of misery so they could appreciate what they were losing.

Too fast, said their grandfather. Who'd of thought a plow and a few drainage tiles could make D-Con and DDT look like chicken feed?

# THE GRANDFATHER

The grandfather was dying of cancer. He sat in his rocking chair all day, holding onto the armrests. When he tried to get up, or if he leaned the wrong way, he screamed.

The boys came to visit him on Saturdays. They couldn't believe anyone could be in so much pain. When he screamed too loud, they went into the kitchen and waited for him to stop. If he didn't, one of them quietly imitated his sounds and the others snickered. But the boys were careful not to let him hear them, even if he was only faking the pain to get their pity.

Their grandfather behaved more strangely with each visit. One day he asked them to put a pulley on the ceiling and to lower a hook to put in his nose and hoist him out of his chair. Another time he yelled, I must shit! but the grown-ups closed the windows so no one could hear him and said, You have not eaten, there is no reason.

When spring came, he said, I am going to die before the weather gets hot. He wanted to stay in bed and to have the house quiet. He asked the boys to come into his bedroom and shake hands with him, but their grip made him scream so loud that they quickly left for the kitchen.

Then a mourning dove built her nest outside his

bedroom window. Her cooing woke him from his fitful naps. He cursed at the bird in his hollow voice.

On their next visit the boys brought their BB gun. One climbed the tree where the mourning dove nested on her eggs. The beak stuck over the edge of the nest. He shot the mourning dove in the throat, and it flapped wildly to the ground. He threw the eggs down for the other boys to smash while the mourning dove fluttered and bled in the grass.

The boys brought the dead bird inside and held it up for their grandfather. They extended their arms toward him, each of them holding part of the bird's wings between his fingers, so he could see that this gift was from all of them.

## A NOTE ON THE TYPE

This book was set in DeVinne, an American
typeface that is actually a recutting by
Gustav Schroeder of French Elzevir. It was
introduced by the Central Type Foundry of
St. Louis in 1889. Named in honor of
Theodore Low DeVinne, whose nine-story
plant, called The Fortress, was the first
building in New York City erected expressly
for printing, the type has a delicate quality
obtained by the contrast between the thick
and thin parts of letters. An enormously
popular type during the early part of this
century, DeVinne combines easy readability
with a nostalgically atmospheric feeling.

Composed by Creative Graphics,
Allentown, Pennsylvania
Printed and bound by The Haddon Craftsmen,
Scranton, Pennsylvania

Photography and typography by
Archie Ferguson